THIS
PRECIOUS
YEAR

by Borghild Dahl

Borghild Dahl

THIS
PRECIOUS
YEAR

E. P. Dutton & Co., Inc., New York

For fifty golden years I have enjoyed the privilege of having students come to me, first in classrooms in high school and college in the Middle West, and later for private instruction in my apartment in New York City. In appreciation for all these hours we spent together, I dedicate to these students this book.

1   *SEPTEMBER*

HELIA got up from the chair she had been occupying for the last quarter of an hour and shook out the crumpled skirt of her blue cotton dress. The sun was pouring in through the row of windows, and the room was uncomfortably hot.

It was far past noon, so afternoon registration ought to be getting under way. Helia wanted to talk over her program with some of her classmates before she went into the registrar's office. The paper-littered desks showed that students had been registering there during the morning, but surely not all of them had finished.

Then a thought struck her. Suppose none of her senior classmates had managed to get back! Suppose the terrible drought and the depression had made it impossible for them to finish college.

Helia walked over to one of the windows and looked out over the windswept campus. There was not a blade of green grass to be seen. Even the tall buckthorn hedge, which had been so dense with leaves that it was like a solid wall, dividing the athletic field from the main campus, now stood brown and gaunt, a mere row of sticks. Like the country district in which she lived, Wheat

City had been stricken by a plague of grasshoppers as well as by drought. Although the bank of trees toward the north had escaped the grasshoppers, there was but a sparse covering of leaves on the branches, and these were so pale and shriveled that the blue sky showed through. Only the two lilac bushes flanking the entrance to the chapel, and the evergreen just outside Nil's heating plant, showed even a semblance of their original beauty. And this must have been due to the care and constant watering Old Nils had given them all summer.

The lilac bushes were said to have been brought from Norway as tiny slips by one of the early pioneers, who migrated from Trondheim, which in the early days had been known as Nidaros. When these early settlers founded their school, they named it Nidaros College. Helia had heard that Trondheim had always been a city of lilacs. In the spring, people approaching it had known exactly how far away they were by the strength of the scent of the blossoms in full bloom.

The lilac bushes by the chapel had been tended as carefully as though the very existence of the college depended upon their survival, but now their leaves lacked luster and were coated with dust. As for the evergreen outside Old Nils' heating plant—Helia knew that if Nils had had to choose between seeing that the tree, brought over from his own village in Norway, was watered, or getting enough to drink himself, the evergreen would have won out. But in spite of his care, there were blotches of rust among the green branches.

Just then she saw Old Nils crossing the campus with Mike, the boxer, at his heels, and the sight reassured her. Old Nils and Mike were as much a part of Nidaros College as the chapel bell. As far as anyone knew, Nils had been there ever since the first Norwegian pioneers had established the little Lutheran academy in Dakota. Nils was ageless; he was the first person every student looked for when he returned to the campus. Although the old man could not have amassed a fortune of any size in his humble position as janitor and handyman, he was never known to refuse to give a boy or girl in need a loan, or an outright gift. And it was said that he sensed financial difficulties without being told.

Although Mike had come to Nidaros later than Nils, he was just as much a part of the college. He roamed about the four buildings at will, attended chapel with infallible punctuality, and went to the class of his choice whenever he felt the need of any particular instruction. At chapel and in the classroom his behavior was beyond reproach. He was even said to cross his paws at exactly the right moment in prayer, and he stood up with the students during the singing of hymns. In class, he had never been known to cause the slightest disturbance, and his attendance was so well accepted that his presence was scarcely noticed. He had a particular liking for cooking lessons in the home economics department.

Old Nils opened the door of the stack house that held the heating plant, and he and Mike disappeared inside. Helia knew exactly what happened next. Nils would put the paper bag he had been carrying on the rickety table close to the door. It contained his afternoon snack, and a pint of coffee, and two lumps of sugar, one for him and one for Mike. Mother Gunda never forgot to have it ready at this time of day.

Mother Gunda, who did the general work in the kitchen,

took almost as much interest in the students as Nils. She would often smuggle out a meal to some student who was on short rations, and then, being a very devout woman, quiet her conscience by reasoning that this act of charity would be credited to the college administrators.

Helia was brought back to the present by a cheerful voice saying, "Well, if it isn't Helia Singstad!"

She turned from the window to see Lillemor Hegg.

"We were so worried you wouldn't be able to make it!" Lillemor exclaimed, and gave her an affectionate hug.

Then another pair of arms were about her. It was Bodil Anderson. Bodil and Lillemor lived some miles north of Helia's village, and she had had no news of them all summer.

"I was beginning to think that no one was coming back this year," Helia said.

"That's how we felt, too," Bodil said. "Except for the Otness boys, we haven't come across anyone else in the senior class except you."

Bodil, always small and slender, looked even more frail this fall, and her brown eyes looked larger than ever. She had never been exuberant, but there had been a calm assurance about her that was lacking now.

"Things were bad this summer," Bodil said. "We couldn't do any fall plowing for fear of raising more dust. It seemed out of the question for me to come back."

"But I told her," Lillemor put in quickly, "that moping at home wasn't going to stop the drought or help her parents either. Things are bad at our farm, too, and if it weren't for the pigs I wouldn't be here at this very moment."

This struck them as funny, and they all started laughing.

"I don't mean I rode on the back of a pig to get here," said Lillemor, her blue eyes sparkling.

"She means that the money they got for selling the pigs helped to make it possible for her to come," Bodil explained.

Lillemor told Helia how their sow had had piglets early in the spring, but because of the drought there was nothing but sow thistle growing on the place and her father was afraid they wouldn't be able to raise the litter. Lillemor had worked as a substitute waitress for a few days in a restaurant in her home town, and had noticed that food was often wasted. At her mother's suggestion she asked the owner of the restaurant if he would let her have the scraps for their pigs, and Lillemor and her oldest brother took turns riding their bicycle into town to collect them.

"From now on," Lillemor finished, "pigs are my favorite animal."

"But how did you get to Wheat City if you didn't ride on one of the pigs?" asked Helia.

"The Otness boys were over at our place one evening, and they invited me to ride back with them. They wanted to be here early in hopes of getting some kind of a job. Otherwise they won't be able to finish this year. You know, it's the same all over the state. Sow thistle is our only crop."

"And Lillemor," Bodil added, "asked the Otness boys if they would give me a lift, too."

"Well, I wanted company. You see, even the pigs couldn't carry me through the whole year. So I asked the boys if they thought girls could find some sort of a job, too."

"My folks are old," Bodil said, "and my father is troubled with rheumatism. But Lillemor made me see that if I could manage to finish my senior year I could get a job teaching and do more for them in the long run than by staying at home. After all, there's almost nothing to do there, with all the animals sent away and no crop to harvest."

"And did you get jobs?" Helia asked.

"We did," said Bodil. "Both of us, and close together, too."

"But what about your classes?" Helia asked.

"That's what we've been seeing about all morning."

"You shouldn't have much trouble," Helia said. "Weren't you just about registered last spring?"

"Yes," Lillemor said, "but that was before we knew we were going to work for our room and board. It isn't what subjects we're going to take but how we're going to fit them in."

"The Mrs. Swift I work for is all system," Bodil said. "She lives and moves like a machine."

"That should make it easy," Helia said. "You'll know exactly when you work and when you'll be free."

"In theory it sounds fine," Bodil admitted. "Rise at six. Prepare breakfast, which must be served at seven sharp. Beds made, dishes washed, and kitchen tidied up by seven-thirty. My first class starts at eight, and it takes at least ten minutes to get here even if I run."

"You don't know how lucky you are," Lillemor said, laughing. "System is a word which my Mrs. Little has never included in her vocabulary. She and her husband and their three children believe in living by inspiration and enjoying every minute of it. So when eight o'clock rolls around and I'm supposed to be at school, the family is barely seated at the table."

"And so?"

"And so, when I return just after eleven o'clock after my three morning classes, the dining room and kitchen look as though a cyclone had struck them."

"But you haven't started yet," Helia reminded her. "How do you know it's going to be like that?"

"Because I spent last night there."

"Will you stay?" Helia asked.

"Of course I'll stay. I want to graduate, don't I?"

"Maybe you could get better jobs," Helia suggested.

"No," Bodil said. "Mrs. Swift is really just as anxious for me to get my own work done as hers. She put a desk and study lamp in my room. My only worry is whether I'm going to be able to stay awake to make use of the time I'll have in the evening."

"And you?" Helia asked Lillemor.

"Mrs. Little is kindness itself. And her three children tag after me wherever I go. They are darlings and want to help me, but instead they keep me from my work. Mrs. Little wants me to attend school, but she doesn't quite know how to call off the attention everyone is showering on me." Lillemor's broad, good-humored face was wreathed in smiles. It was easy to see why the children liked her so well.

"Anyhow, you both are back," said Helia. "As for me—"

Bodil interrupted her, exclaiming, "Oh, it's almost two o'clock! I should be in Mrs. Swift's kitchen stirring up a cake to serve the ladies who are coming to tea." She looked a little anxious.

"You can see we've lost no time in getting started," said Lillemor. She and Bodil were laughing at their plight as they left the room.

Helia sat down at a desk close to the door, where the slight draft made the heat more bearable. She felt almost guilty to be sitting idle while her two friends were rushing back to their jobs.

It must have taken a lot of courage and will power for them to come back this year, she thought. Lillemor's parents were renters, and paid for their house with part of each year's crop. With nothing to harvest, it would be difficult for them to remain on the place at all; however, all the farmers were equally hard hit, and the landlord could not easily find tenants. As for Bodil's folks, who were better off, they owned their quarter-section of land, but there had been a lot of sickness in the family.

"Well, if the lady herself hasn't arrived!"

Helia looked up as the two Otness brothers strode into the room and came up to her to shake hands. They were tall, big-boned and blue-eyed, with weather-beaten faces and deeply tanned hands. Wilhelm and Oivind were exactly the same height and build, and might have been taken for twins, though there was a year between them. They lived about fifteen miles from Helia's home town of Prairie Village, and she had known them as long as she could remember. The Otnesses were a rather boisterous family, but kind and hard-working. With ten children, there had never been too much money to go round, and during the drought it must have required good management to feed so many.

"When did you get in?" Wilhelm asked Helia.

"Just a little while ago. The Olsons were taking a load of cattle to be farmed out in Minnesota, so I got a ride with them."

"Peter Leegaard told us you didn't decide to come back until the last minute," Wilhelm said with a twinkle in his eye. "And you can bet he didn't shed any tears at the news."

Helia felt her cheeks grow hot. "Bodil and Lillemor told me you've been here some time," she said, trying to hide her confusion.

"Yes, we came down before the rush to be sure of a job." It was Oivind who volunteered this information.

"And did you get one?"

"Did we!" they chorused, and Wilhelm continued:

"Most modern apartment in town. Carpeting from wall to wall. A canary singing in the window amid a bower of blooming plants. And you should see our kitchen. Modern sink, hot and cold water, icebox—"

Helia interrupted him. "That's enough of that fairy tale. Now tell me the truth."

"But it is the truth. The whole truth, and nothing but."

"The whole truth?" said Helia.

The Otness boys looked at each other. "You tell her," Wilhelm said.

"No, you were the one that got the job for us," said Oivind.

"All right," said Wilhelm, "since you must know, we're working for Emerson's."

"The funeral parlor?"

"That's right. Everyone will know sooner or later anyway."

"But don't you mind—I mean, isn't it creepy and scary?" Helia asked haltingly.

"Scary? What is there to be scared of?" Wilhelm asked brusquely.

"Anyhow, we'll get used to it. All we have to do is to drive out when Emerson's gets a call and pick up the . . . the . . ."

His brother interrupted. "We didn't have much of a choice, and this was the job that gave us most time for study. Our marks haven't been anything to brag about, and with the drought and all making everything harder, we decided we'd really have to buckle down this year."

"But we want to explain to our folks what we're doing before they get the news secondhand. Mother is a little squeamish."

"I won't tell," Helia promised, but after the Otness boys had gone she found it hard to concentrate on her schedule. Oivind and Wilhelm had always seemed rather easygoing and not particularly ambitious. Would she have the courage or the stamina to keep going as they were? Like Lillemor, they were making a tremendous effort to complete their education.

She found herself wondering about Peter Leegaard. She had heard that Peter had remained in Wheat City for a while after school closed, but no one had said anything more about what he was doing. She wished she had asked the Otness boys.

"And what's troubling you, Helia? You look worried."

Helia started. It was Peter himself. He was as tall as the Otness brothers but much more slender, and had none of their healthy outdoor color.

"What's worrying you?" Peter asked again, pushing back the lock of blond hair that insisted on falling over his forehead.

"I was worrying about you," Helia said, and laughed. He wouldn't believe it, so she might as well tell the truth.

"I just met Wilhelm and Oivind," he said, "and they told me you were in here. I was beginning to think that perhaps you had changed your mind again and weren't coming back this year."

Helia could feel herself blushing at the real concern in his voice.

"Why don't you sit down and tell me about yourself?" she suggested.

As he sat facing her, she could see how thin he was.

"I didn't go home this summer," he said. "The house is empty, and there was nothing to take me there."

How could such a fine fellow as Peter have such a shiftless father? Helia wondered. Peter was one of the best students on the campus, just as he had been in high school. It was because Professor Jensen had taken an interest in him that he had been able to get into college, for his father took no responsibility for him at all. Though there had been only a few test tubes to work with in high school, Peter had shown a remarkable aptitude for chemistry.

In his first year at college, he had been one of the students to whom Mother Gunda smuggled food, but since then he seemed to have managed. He had shoveled coal down at the railroad freight yards, washed dishes in the restaurant, and taken any jobs that were available.

"I'm in clover now," he said. "Chief engineer at the

White Laundry. I help pack the clothes after they've been washed and dried, and if there are rush orders I help deliver them. Mr. White is one of the finest men anyone could work for."

"And Peter Leegaard is one of the finest workers he could ever get."

"Now you're poking fun at me," said Peter. But his cheeks were pink back to his ears, and Helia could see he was pleased even though he pretended not to be.

"Mother Gunda offered me a chance to wait on table at breakfast, but I'm giving that job to Jon Finstad. I get enough money at the laundry to cover all my meals."

He started to tell her about some of their other friends who had found jobs. One group of boys had rented a partly furnished house and contracted with the local bakery for day-old bread and cake. They delivered groceries on Saturday and got food for that, too, and for fuel they were clearing out the timber that had dried during the drought. Helia was so interested in what he was saying that she hardly noticed how time had passed until a girl's voice said, "You're Helia Singstad, aren't you? They're asking about you at the registrar's office."

Peter jumped out of his seat. "I should have told you, Helia. The sun is so hot in this room in the afternoon that they decided to make up the programs on the other side of the hall. This is Marion Fletcher, Helia. I . . . I have to go now," and he hurried out the door.

"He's so shy," Marion Fletcher said. "But simply a dear. I met him this summer when he came into Father's bank. He was working at some laundry. I'll walk with you to the registrar's office."

Helia looked at her. So this was the daughter of the wealthy Millard Fletcher, whose name appeared so often on the society page of the Wheat City *Daily*. Marion Fletcher was wearing a rose-colored suit, a large white hat, and spotless white gloves. She belonged to a group so foreign to Helia that she might have come from a different world.

"Father insists that I attend college in Wheat City this year," Marion went on in her slight drawl, "although I simply can't imagine why. He says it's the depression and the drought and that it's only right to keep the money at home. Father has such queer notions about money. I suppose it's because he spends so much time in a bank."

Up to now Helia had sat tongue-tied, too impressed to be able to say anything. But surprise freed her tongue. "Don't you like going to college?" she asked.

"Oh, dear, yes," Marion Fletcher said. "At least, I did. We had such a good crowd at Smith. It breaks my heart to think what I'll be missing this winter."

"But we always have fun here at Nidaros, too," Helia managed to say.

Marion shrugged her shoulders. Then, as if she realized her rudeness, she said, "Ever so many of the Wheat City young people are going to Nidaros College this winter, so I'm sure we'll make out. Besides, there is Dr. Winters."

Helia looked surprised, and Marion continued:

"Haven't you heard? He's the new young professor of English literature from New York. I haven't met him yet but I've seen him. He's taken a room on our street, and he's very attractive."

This bit of news greatly excited Helia. A young professor from the East! She was majoring in English and hoped to teach it next year if she was fortunate enough to get a position, so she would be in his classes.

When she reached the registrar's office, Professor Gortvedt, the head of the placement bureau, helped her make out her program.

"I think you should take another year of chemistry," he told her.

"But I don't like science," Helia protested. "I'd much rather take an extra course in literature." That would mean she'd have the new professor in two classes, she thought.

"We're hoping to be admitted to the North Central Association of Colleges with full accreditation this year, but in the meantime we're still at a disadvantage in securing positions for our students. The more subjects you can offer as teaching majors and minors, the better chance you will have to get a teaching position. And you already have a strong English major."

"Oh, all right," Helia said. "But I wish I liked chemistry as much as Peter Leegaard does. He practically lives for the privilege of handling the laboratory equipment."

"Perhaps he will give you a hand now and then," Professor Gortvedt said.

Helia felt her cheeks burn, but Professor Gortvedt didn't notice. He was too set and staid to be aware of anything but getting students ready to teach.

Half an hour later, up in her room at the dormitory, Helia pulled off her dress and lay down on the bed. The air was stifling, the only window faced west. How long was it since a single cloud had appeared in the sky to shut out the blazing sun? she wondered.

It had been a long day. She could scarcely realize that she had eaten breakfast in the farm kitchen. It had been a tearful farewell even though everyone, including her youngest brother Norman, was happy that she was going back to college.

Helia would never forget the morning she knew that she was going to return. They had just finished breakfast and were still sitting at the table when her mother said she had something to tell them.

By that time Helia had given up all hope of going back to Nidaros College. Since early spring the drought had grown steadily worse, and when harvest time came there was nothing in the fields but thistles. Sand lay like snow on the roadside. The wind blew up clouds of dust until it grew so dark that cars often had to turn on their head-lights in the middle of the day. Helia was haunted by the fear that she would have to give up college. She knew how carefully her parents had had to plan to send her to Nidaros the last three years, but by tacit consent the sub-ject was never mentioned.

Their cattle had been sent away in the middle of August because there was nothing to feed them. Only one cow was left, and there was barely enough feed for her. They had applied to the government for feed grants for their horse. It was cheaper to use him than the car, which was getting old and had to be spared for emergencies. The boys walked to school. They no longer had butter for their bread, but no one ever spoke about the changes the drought had made in their lives.

They were all the more surprised that morning after breakfast when Mother said she had an announcement to make. She left the table and came back carrying the copper kettle that she had brought to Dakota all the way from Norway. She sat down beside her husband and then she began to speak.

"As you know," she said, "I have always hoped to return to Norway once in my lifetime to visit my sisters. And I still have that hope. But there is something else that must be taken care of first, and that is for Helia to finish college. We have all been concerned, even though we haven't said anything."

Then her mother took off the lid of the copper coffee kettle and began to take out the quarters, dimes, nickels, pennies, and a few dollar bills that filled it. She put them on the empty bread plate by Helia's place.

"I counted this money one night when you were all sleeping," she said. "There are one hundred and ten dollars and fifty-nine cents. There will always be time for my trip to Norway, and when I go I want to feel that everything is well at home."

Helia's eyes burned with tears as she thought of the sacrifice her mother was making, though she pretended that she was doing it only for her peace of mind. And everything that followed was wonderful, too. Her oldest brother, Theodore, said that he hoped to pick up odd jobs around town after school and give her his small savings. Norman ran for his piggy bank and counted out of it twenty-eight cents which he added to the heap on the plate. And finally Edvard, who was slower and less articulate than the rest, offered to sell his ice skates, but Helia told him that would not be necessary.

Helia got up from the bed, and started to unpack her clothes. She must be up bright and early the next morning. With everyone pulling for her at home, she was certainly going to do her best to make good use of this precious year, her last one at college.

"NOW, if you just give yourself time and put down exactly what you see, you'll have no trouble at all with your chemistry experiments." Peter, usually so bashful and hesitant, spoke with absolute authority.

This was a new Peter, one Helia had not known.

"If you knew how much I worry about chemistry," she complained, "you wouldn't act as though all I have to do is to push my pen in the right direction."

"I told you you're getting along well," Peter said.

"If I have to teach this subject, I'll resign," Helia retorted.

"Oh, no, you won't. You've got better stuff in you than that."

"The only thing I'm dead sure of is what H_2O stands for. And if this drought keeps up any longer, I'm not sure I'll remember what that is."

Peter tossed his head back so far that his unruly lock of hair almost reached his left eyebrow, and laughed as Helia had seldom heard him.

"You can laugh," she said, "but if I fail in a single subject this year, I'm sunk."

"So are the rest of us. But we aren't going to fail—

neither you nor I. And I'm going to continue to coach you in chemistry."

At least, thought Helia, Early English Literature is going to be much easier. And exciting, too, since it was going to be taught by a young professor from the East.

She only hoped that she could measure up to his high standards.

When Dr. Winters entered the classroom, Helia thought that she had never seen so romantic and distinguished a teacher. He was slender, of medium height, with brown eyes and wavy brown hair. As he placed his books and papers on the desk, she could see that his nails were carefully manicured. And as for his clothes, Helia had never seen such a well-cut suit.

She was impressed by his voice, too, which was low and cultivated. Everything about Dr. Winters reflected distinction. And when he read to them, she sat spellbound.

After a few days, however, it began to dawn on her that she did not really understand what Dr. Winters was talking about. In chemistry it was entirely different. When anything came up that she didn't understand, all she had to do was to turn to Peter for guidance, and he would go over each item step by step and in great detail. To be sure, chemistry was a much more definite subject than literature. Yet if Dr. Winters would only give the class some way to interpret the various selections, it would be easier to understand them. English was a difficult subject for some of the students who came from homes where they spoke Norwegian.

Helia met frequently with Lillemor and Bodil to talk over this problem.

"I love to listen to Dr. Winters," Bodil said, "but I don't remember anything afterward and I come away from class in a daze."

Helia tried to defend their professor by saying that it was because of their limited background that they were not able to appreciate all he had to offer. But then Lillemor said it was his business to make up for whatever they had been denied. "I think every teacher ought to find out just how much help a student needs and then give it to him."

"I don't dare to think what's going to happen when we come to written examinations," Bodil said.

College had been in session about three weeks when Dr. Winters called for the first written test. This included questions from Old and Middle English, and although Helia was fairly sure of herself when she arrived in class, her heart sank when she saw what was being asked of her:

Why did *Beowulf* survive when much of Old English literature must have been lost?

Describe Chaucer's personality as revealed in one of his works.

Give specific examples of how the English language was influenced by the Norman Conquest.

The third question she could answer fairly well, but the first two drew an almost complete blank. She had committed to memory as best she could the works of various authors, but she had not stopped to consider what their philosophy might be, nor did she know much about the historical background of English literature.

Usually English had been her best subject, and with

the added incentive of the handsome young Dr. Winters as her instructor, she had hopes for success in this class at least. But instead of sticking to the text, so that she could hold forth at length on what she had read and committed to memory, Dr. Winters asked the students to explain some small detail they had entirely overlooked. Or he took it for granted that their horizons extended far beyond that of the high school or college classroom. When he questioned them about Winchester in England, where King Alfred was supposed to have lived, he almost expected them to have traveled through England, and be familiar with every stick and stone there.

It did not help Helia's fast-growing feeling of inferiority to realize that Marion Fletcher seemed to be able to discuss, indefinitely and with complete assurance, any subject Dr. Winters saw fit to bring up. When the test papers came back, Marion had a high grade; Helia had barely passed.

Two days later, Wilhelm Otness stopped her outside class.

"What's the matter with you?" he asked. "You used to be our shining light in English class and now you sit like a scared mouse in a corner."

Helia felt like crying. "I—I just don't seem to understand what he expects of us," she managed to say.

"None of us do," said Wilhelm. "You should see what he wrote on my test paper."

Helia looked at him in surprise. "You mean you didn't pass?"

"Pass! If I could have gotten a worse grade, the system would have had to be done over."

Helia swallowed hard. She was ashamed of her feelings, but this news comforted her greatly.

"But I didn't take it lying down," Wilhelm said. "That is, I didn't quarrel with Dr. Winters or complain about the grade. All I did was to ask Dr. Willoughby Winters to please come down to our level—Oh," he added quickly, "I wasn't that insulting. But I told him that we lived out here on a frontier and we didn't have the advantage of visiting the places that were so familiar to him, and we didn't have the background he seemed to think we had."

"And what did he say?" Helia asked.

"He admitted that it took considerable adjusting for him to get used to living on the frontier with us savages. He didn't use that word exactly, but I got what he meant. And I think he got what I meant too."

"Aren't you afraid he may be down on you for talking to him like that?" Helia asked.

"Not at all. I couldn't do worse than I have. I'm here to get an education, or as much of one as I can. And I'm not going to let anyone scare me out of it, if I can help it."

As Helia walked upstairs to her room in the dormitory, she wondered why she had ever thought that Wilhelm had no spirit. She was finding out a lot of things this year that weren't included in the textbooks.

The following evening the buzzer in her room told her she was wanted downstairs. She found Peter Leegaard and Wilhelm Otness waiting for her in the north parlor. They wanted to talk to her in confidence.

Wilhelm told Helia that her name had been suggested as one of the candidates for the Homecoming Queen. He and Peter wanted to act as her campaign managers and do everything they could to get her elected.

"I thought at first we'd have clear sailing," Wilhelm said. "But this year the town bunch are getting into the running too, and they're backing Marion Fletcher."

Peter put his hand lightly on Helia's shoulder. "We always intended you to be our queen," he said in a low voice.

Wilhelm's jaw set hard. "Anyway, we'll give those city slickers a run for their money," he said.

That night Helia found it hard to get to sleep. Every girl at the college wanted to be Homecoming Queen in the fall of her senior year. Six girls were put up as candidates. The one who got the most votes became queen; the next highest was the maid of honor; and the other four were court attendants.

Helia knew she was popular, and she had to admit that she had almost taken it for granted that she would be elected. She had pictured herself wearing the royal robes and being crowned in the chapel while the college band played "Hail to the Chief." Accompanied by her attendants, wearing beautiful evening dresses, she would be driven around the campus in a buggy pulled by four honor guards—a campus made bright by an immense bonfire.

On Saturday morning there would be a big parade, and she would sit on a beautifully decorated float, surrounded by her attendants. They would go down the town's main street and back to the campus for the Homecoming football game. There she would occupy the box of honor and be hailed by the crowd. Nidaros College would, of course, defeat its opponents and she would be hailed as the inspiration for the victory.

That night, at the alumni banquet in the college gymnasium, she would be seated on the dais with the president of the college, the president of the Alumni Association, and Peter Leegaard, who was president of the student body. Toasts would be drunk to all the former Homecoming Queens, and a special toast would be drunk to her alone.

On Sunday, she would still wear her royal robes, and at the morning church services the visitors who had come to town for the occasion would congratulate her and say how proud they were. Perhaps even her family might be able to come.

If she were only the maid of honor or one of the attendants—well, it wouldn't really matter whether they were there or not.

Finally the rising bell shrilled its warning, and Helia jumped out of bed after a sleepless night. After all, she still had to attend classes. And it was much more important—hard as it might be to believe on that particular morning—for her to graduate than to be voted queen.

At a mass meeting of the student body, Roscoe Woodburn spoke for the town group.

"Nidaros is a small, struggling college," he said, "and it needs all the support that can come its way. This support can be multiplied greatly if the daughter of one of our outstanding citizens is chosen to represent the student body at the Homecoming. I need not mention how helpful it would be to the financial welfare of the college if the town's leading banker became interested in Nidaros."

One of the new members of the junior class was just as convincing. "We want the parade this year to be the best ever. And just imagine the appearance Marion Fletcher can make in the clothes her people will be able to deck her out in."

Since Peter was presiding, he was supposed to represent the whole student body and to stay neutral. His face flushed as he listened, but he said nothing. At that moment Wilhelm rose to his feet.

"I'm not good at making speeches," he said, soberly. "And it's been a hard year for us farmers. If Helia is elected queen, it's true she won't have the expensive clothes you town people are able to afford. But up to this year, you never cared whether we even had a Homecoming."

There was some applause, but it was not so loud as that which greeted the first two speakers.

The next day the student body met and the votes were counted. Peter Leegaard presided to see that all was done properly. Two blindfolded freshmen took each vote from the ballot box, two sophomores read the name, and Peter recorded it.

Marion Fletcher. Marion Fletcher. Helia Singstad.

The counting went on and on. As Helia listened, she realized that Marion's name was being mentioned twice to her once.

It wasn't fair, she told herself bitterly. These people came in and took over, when they hadn't even admitted a year earlier that Nidaros College existed, or cared whether it existed. Her eyes smarted, but she was determined that no one would guess her disappointment, Roscoe Woodburn and Marion Fletcher least of all. So when the count was over and the result was announced, she immediately went to congratulate Marion and tell her that she would make a wonderful Homecoming Queen.

But, as soon as the meeting broke up, Helia rushed to her room and locked the door. She threw herself down on the bed and wept until finally she fell asleep.

She was awakened by a knock at her door and got up to answer it. It was a little freshman from across the hall.

"Peter Leegaard is downstairs. He asked me to tell you that he'd like you to come down."

Helia went to the washroom and dashed cold water over her face. Then she went back to her room to comb her hair and put on a clean blouse before she went downstairs.

"I thought we might take a walk," Peter said.

That was all, and they started out. They walked from one end of town to the other without speaking until they stopped at an ice-cream parlor for a Coke.

Sitting opposite her, Peter spoke at last. "We were disappointed today," he said simply. "There was nothing we could do. But never mind, Helia. All of us who know you feel *you* are really our queen."

It wasn't so much what he said but what he felt that counted, and on the way home Helia resolved to be a good sport about it.

On the day before the beginning of Homecoming, Helia was closeted in her room, doing her best to alter a rose satin gown that Mrs. Little had given Lillemor. It was both too large and too long, and although Helia had had considerable training at home with her needle, she was having trouble making the dress fit Lillemor who had won a place as one of the attendants. Helia was determined that Lillemor's dress should be as fine as anyone's there. As for herself, she was wearing her green voile. It had had many washings but they were careful ones.

While she worked, Bodil came into the room carrying a fairly good-sized box.

"Here's a package for you, Helia. The mailman just left it and the Dean signed for it."

Helia dropped the sash she was tying around Lillemor's waist and seized the box. It could only be from home, but what could her family be sending her? They had written that they were proud to learn she had been chosen maid of honor but that because the trip would use up so much gas it seemed best for them not to come to the Homecoming. After all, Helia had been away only a little more than a month, although her mother said that it seemed much longer. But she had not mentioned a package.

Helia started to open it. True to her training, she carefully untied the knots in the string so that it came out in one piece, and rolled it into a tiny ball. She removed the paper without tearing it, and saved the ribbon tied around the white box. Finally the box was ready to be opened.

Helia held her breath. Then, with the utmost care, she lifted the lid. White tissue paper was all she saw at first. But . . . no, it couldn't be. Yes, it was. Her mother's wedding dress. As long as Helia could remember, the dress had been carefully preserved in a sheet at the bottom of her mother's cedar chest—the chest her mother had brought from Norway when she emigrated to America.

With trembling hands Helia took the dress from its tissue wrappings. She had always considered it the loveliest dress she had ever seen. But, as she held it up, she was surprised to see that it had been changed. Instead of a high neck with white ruching on top, it now had a low neckline. The long full sleeves had been removed and there were only suggestions of caps at the shoulders. There were borders of brilliant beads around the neck, around the tiny cap sleeves, at the shoulder and around the belt.

A slip of paper fell out of the box as she removed the dress. Helia stooped to pick it up. Tears gathered in her eyes as she read:

We all hope the dress will fit you, and since I have sewed your dresses all along, the measurements should be accurate. Your father and all three of the boys gave their opinion of the dress, and their suggestions were good. Theodore helped me rip up the little bead bag you will remember that I had for years, and it was Norman's idea that we should use the extra cloth from the sleeves as a band for your hair. Edvard said that the beads should be sewn on this too.

Her mother did not say how hard she had worked, nor did she mention that it had not been easy for her to cut up this most precious of all her treasures.

"Put it on," Bodil said.

But they hadn't seen it all. There was another layer of tissue paper and below it was the original slip that had been made for the dress.

Bodil and Lillemor helped her try it on, for Helia's hands shook so that she fumbled everything. After she was dressed in her new gown, her hair combed and the band tied on it, Bodil said, "Now look in the mirror. If Marion Fletcher can do anything better than that, I would like to see it." And as Helia saw herself in the glass, she wondered if that reflection could possibly be hers.

That night Helia had washed her hair and was waiting for it to dry when there was a light tap at the door. I hope whoever it is will make it brief, she thought.

She opened the door and was amazed to find Marion Fletcher standing in the hall. She was too astonished to do anything but stare at her.

"May I come in?" Marion asked.

"Of course," Helia said.

There was only one chair, so she herself sat on the bed and waited for Marion to speak. But Marion found it difficult to begin.

"When I was—when they chose me as Homecoming Queen, well, it didn't occur to me that I had to do anything but wait to be crowned."

Helia said nothing.

"But it seems that there is—there are traditions to be taken into consideration."

Still Helia waited.

"This is a Norwegian school—"

"That isn't so," said Helia. "We're as American as any college in the United States."

"Yes, well, but I'm supposed to say something about the Norwegians, and I've been to the library—"

"No one expects you to say anything about the Norwegians unless you want to," said Helia. "We aren't any more a Norwegian school than Harvard or Yale is English.

But it's true that Nidaros was established by pioneers from Norway."

"I tried to do some reading at the library," Marion said, "but I got all confused. There were stories about Leif Ericson and a man named Cleng Peerson, and there was something about the Restoration, but I thought that happened in England."

Helia laughed. "I guess you tried to cover too much ground in too short a time. The *Restoration* was the name of the boat that carried the first Norwegian pioneers to America. It was even smaller than the *Mayflower*."

"Do you think," said Marion, "that is—would you give me a few suggestions about what I'm supposed to say in my coronation speech?"

Helia winced. It was bad enough to have lost the election to Marion without being expected to help her with her coronation speech. But she had been elected Marion's maid of honor, her chief attendant. And besides, as she was the one who had been there longer, wasn't she responsible for upholding the traditions of the college?

"All right," Helia said finally. "I'll try to do what I can for you."

Marion's face relaxed. "My dad wouldn't be fit to live with if I made a fiasco of my speech tomorrow. Especially since he had a wonderful purple cape and a crown made up for me in Chicago."

Helia had all she could do to control a flare of jealous anger. Roscoe Woodburn and the rest had been right. One of their chief reasons for backing Marion was that she was going to make such an elegant appearance.

Biting her lip to keep the bitter words from spilling out,

Helia began to tell Marion about the traditions and the history of Nidaros College. Once Marion got the general idea, the two worked steadily and easily together, and before Helia realized it the hands of her alarm clock registered a quarter of twelve.

"Well, I guess that's about all I can do for you," she said, getting up.

Marion got up too. "Dad will read me the riot act for staying out so late, but I'd rather have him do that than face him without a speech. You've been awfully good, Helia, considering that—well—"

"That's all right," Helia said, but she couldn't make herself say any more.

The following morning she met Peter and the two Otness boys on the campus. "Will you explain to Marion about the shield?" Wilhelm said. "We three stayed up until all hours last night making it out of pasteboard and crepe paper. We're using the Norwegian shield with the gold crown and gold lion against a red background, and we're using the American eagle, also gold, against a blue background. We thought that would be symbolic for this year, because of the drought and there not being a cloud in the sky."

Helia smiled. "I'll do my best," she promised.

As she made her way to the chapel to rehearse the coronation, she decided that being maid of honor entailed a good deal more than she had thought it would. As she was standing looking at the throne, Peter joined her.

"The closer the time comes, the more jittery I get," he told her.

"What are you jittery about now?" asked Helia. "Your

speech, when you place the crown on Marion's head?"

"It's not the speech, although goodness knows I'm no orator. It's putting the crown on that I'm worried about."

"That should be simple," Helia said. "All you have to do is to make sure it's on straight."

"That's just it. How do I know it won't slip back on her neck, or lop over one ear, or fall right off?"

Helia burst out laughing. "Marion has a head of good heavy hair," she assured him, "and it's carefully waved. That should hold the crown all right."

"Yes, well, you know, my father and I living alone together for so many years—and with no woman around to tell us what to do—"

Though she laughed, Helia felt genuinely sorry for Peter. In spite of his unusual maturity and competence, there was a kind of unprotected quality about him that made people's hearts go out to him.

"I tell you what," she said after a short pause. "I'll ask Marion to meet you in the little anteroom in front of the chapel, and you can practice crowning her there. She'll probably be glad to have the opportunity of doing a little extra practicing."

Peter's face brightened. "Do you really think so?"

"I do. And if it will make you feel any better, I'll be on hand to help."

By this time they had reached the chapel for the rehearsal. Nearly everyone else had arrived, and the Dean, Miss Estvold, announced briskly that they would not wait for stragglers. She began her instructions at once, with the information that the playing of "The War March of the Priests" from *Athalie* would be the signal for the royal equipage to make its appearance on the platform. She was determined that everything should go well that evening, and she drilled them thoroughly.

Helia took her time getting dressed that evening. Even though she was not going to wear the royal robes, she was wearing the most beautiful dress she had ever owned, and she could not resist a last look in her mirror before she left the dormitory.

Though everyone was at a fever pitch of excitement in the anteroom of the chapel, there was no confusion, since everyone knew exactly what to do. When the band struck up, the attendants, though trembling, went their way. The rest of the procession followed them slowly, just as Dean Estvold had instructed them. Helia had to adjust the queen's heavy train several times, but nothing went actually wrong.

When the music stopped at last, Peter came forward. With his back turned to the audience, and addressing the queen, he made his speech. In loud, clear tones, he stated that Marion had been the choice of the majority of the student body, and, as the successful candidate, had earned the right to be crowned their monarch during Homecoming. He described her activities as ruler, and at the conclusion of his speech he placed the crown on her head.

Helia heaved a sigh of relief. He had done it perfectly.

With her crown on her head, and sitting on her throne, Marion had just begun to speak when there was a slight rustle in the audience. Then, at full speed down the main aisle, came Mike, bounding as he went. He stopped just in front of Marion, and wagged his tail.

The royal attendants gasped and so did Peter. There was a general movement in the audience.

For a moment Helia just stood staring. Mike would ruin

the ceremony if he was left to wander at will, and she was almost inclined to let him. What if he did detract from Marion's hour of triumph? It was none of her affair.

But she knew that it was. She was Marion's chief attendant, and she would be ashamed of herself forever if she gave in to such an unworthy temptation.

She walked over to Mike and caught him firmly by the collar. Then she pulled him over to the seat she would occupy and pushed him under it.

"Stay there!" she whispered.

After a short silence, Marion proceeded with her speech. Although her voice trembled a little, Helia had to admit that she did well. Marion must have an unusual memory, she thought, for she gave almost verbatim everything they had talked over in the dormitory the night before.

When Marion had finished, the band broke into a thunderous "Hail to the Chief" and there was a rush forward from the audience.

The first to reach Marion was her mother. She clasped Marion to her and said, "My child. My darling. What a wonderful queen you are!"

Helia thought she had never seen a woman so elegantly dressed. There were sparkling jewels at her ears, and her fur cape was thrown back enough to show a maroon wool dress.

"You were absolutely dazzling, dear, and I must say those pretty little maids-in-waiting made a most attractive background for you. But whoever allowed that awful dog into the chapel?"

"Well, Marion, you did yourself proud!" A handsome middle-aged man, his hair gray at the temples, came up and kissed her lightly on the forehead. "I didn't think you had it in you to be such a speechmaker."

By now friends were beginning to surround Helia too.

"What do you suppose happened to Mike?" she asked Peter, when he came to congratulate her on her presence of mind. "He never acted like that before."

"I hear he has a new collar. Perhaps he's not used to it yet."

"I hope this won't put an end to his college career," Helia said anxiously.

"You needn't worry," Peter assured her. "Old Nils would never allow anything to happen to Mike. And not even President Presthune opposes Old Nils when he has made up his Norwegian mind about something."

When the evening's festivities were ended, Helia sank down in the chair of her room and sat there without moving. She was completely exhausted, physically and emotionally. The day had seemed interminable, the evening even worse. She felt as though she would never want to move again.

And for what had she expended all this energy? To make a beautiful background for Marion Fletcher as Homecoming Queen. And, at that, she was only one of several with whom she shared this dubious honor. Helia felt her cheeks grow hot with resentment as she remembered Mr. Fletcher's remark.

"I didn't think you had it in you!" No wonder, Mr. Fletcher. Some of the rest of us didn't, either.

Then Helia felt her cheeks grow hot once more, this time with shame. Marion's mother had a right to be proud of her daughter. She had looked beautiful in her purple velvet cape and her crown of sparkling imitation jewels. Both were much more becoming to Marion, with her dark wavy hair and brown eyes, than they would have been to Helia.

Besides, no matter how much praise was lavished on Marion, none of it need distract from Helia's pride in her own appearance. She had been delighted by her reflection in the mirror, and to be envious now was a sorry expression of gratitude to her mother, who had sacrificed the wedding dress that she had preserved so carefully all these years.

As for Marion's speech, she had come to Helia honestly and asked her help. If Helia had objected to helping her, she should have said so at once, instead of being jealous when Marion delivered it so well.

And yet . . .

In years to come it would be Marion Fletcher and not Helia Singstad who would be remembered as the star of this year's Homecoming. It was the successful candidate who enjoyed this heritage. Who cared about who ran against her and was defeated?

This time Helia's eyes filled with tears, and she let them fall.

But what was that commotion outside her window? It was time for lights to be out in the dormitory, and no noise was tolerated on the campus after that.

There was loud singing—a chorus of both boys and girls:

" 'Just a song at twilight—' "

Then "Love's Old Sweet Song."

" 'I love you truly—' "

And now, " 'When I grow too old to dream, I'll have you to remember—' "

Helia sat without moving. This was heaping insult upon injury. Some of the students were serenading the Homecoming Queen, but they didn't have to do it outside her very window.

"Helia! Helia!"

They were shouting her name.

The door opened, and Lillemor and Bodil rushed in.

"Haven't you heard? They're out there! Everybody. They're serenading you." It was Lillemor, her words rushing out and tumbling over each other.

"You were magnificent, Helia. The way you had the presence of mind, while the rest of us were petrified, to pull Mike under your chair. If you hadn't, he would have spoiled the whole coronation."

"Come on! They're waiting for you downstairs." Again Lillemor's words were blurred with excitement and haste.

"But—the Dean. What will she say?"

"Every window in the whole dormitory is lit up. If she has any objections, she certainly hasn't let anyone know." Lillemor pulled Helia out of her chair, took her arm, and started her out of the room.

Helia would never forget the next half-hour. She was immediately seized as soon as she came out of the building. Peter Leegaard and Roscoe Woodburn and two of the juniors made a seat for her with their hands. And then, heading a procession, they began a tour around the campus.

The chorus grew louder and louder: "'For she's a jolly good fellow, which nobody can deny.'"

When finally they returned to the steps of the dormitory, there to greet the crowd was Mike. Never, during his entire career at Nidaros College, had he sent forth such a volley of barks. He barked and barked, and this time no one tried to stop him from running around in circles.

As Helia entered the building, the Dean was there to greet her.

"We were very proud of you tonight," she told Helia. "And I think this is one coronation none of us will ever forget."

3   *NOVEMBER*

IT WAS Thanksgiving Day, and Helia slowly climbed the stairs leading from the dining room to the main floor. She stood for a moment looking into the parlor.

Two bedraggled brown-paper turkeys hung loosely from their pinned perch on one of the draperies in the doorway leading into the hall. A lone streamer of orange crepe paper dangled from the central chandelier. On the table a crumpled paper cup had been left beside a pile of cookie crumbs. If Dean Estvold had not been in such a hurry to catch the late train after the party last night, the clean-up committee would not have dared to make such short shrift of their job.

Helia shivered, though she was wearing a black wool skirt and a gray wool sweater. It was about as unbecoming an outfit as she possessed, but why dress up to moon all day in the dormitory? It might have helped if there had been more heat in the building. But Old Nils was as solicitous of the financial welfare of Nidaros College as he was of that of the individual students, and with most of the students gone for the holidays he would really have liked to turn off the heat altogether.

Marion Fletcher had told her that Dr. Winters was

having Thanksgiving dinner with them. Helia knew the Fletcher mansion only from having passed it, but she let her imagination picture the elegant rooms, the beautifully set table with its gleaming white linen cloth, the shining expensive dishes and brightly polished silver. There would be a turkey and everything to go with it, all served by a smartly dressed maid in a black dress uniform and a white cap and apron.

But why must she spend so much time thinking about Marion Fletcher? She would do better to think about how the three Ronning boys had set out for home.

The Ronning brothers—Bert, a senior, Elmer, a junior, and Lawrence, a freshman—had lined up outside the dormitory yesterday just after lunch, three abreast. On Bert's chest was pinned a green and yellow placard—the school colors—with the words "Nidaros College" in yellow letters on green. Elmer's placard was white, and in heavy black letters it said, "Bound for Home for Thanksgiving." And Lawrence's red placard had white letters which said, "Please Give Us a Lift."

Helia had heard that they had scarcely reached the top of Jenkins Hill on the outskirts of town before someone bound for their part of Iowa had picked them up.

They hadn't felt sorry for themselves and moped around because they were homesick. They were resourceful. They had wanted to go home and had done something about it.

Well, she couldn't get home, but she could use these three days to catch up on all sorts of work. There was that paper on Charlemagne for World History, and she might even be able to do some reading for her English courses.

And she'd go right upstairs and put on the plaid wool skirt and pretty red flannel shirt her mother had made her and which she kept for Sundays. She always felt dressed up in them, and happy.

"Helia! Helia! Where are you?"

There was only one person who pronounced her name like that—stressing the first syllable so that it sounded like two. But what was Peter Leegaard doing on the campus this morning? He and the Otness boys had been so vague about their Thanksgiving plans that Helia had taken it for granted they were working, as Bodil and Lillemor apparently were.

"Helia! Helia!"

She ran out into the hall, like a child who has been deserted in the dark and has just heard a welcome voice.

"Are you ready to come home with us?" Peter asked, smiling.

"Home?" said Helia. "Who said anything about home?"

Peter took her arm. "Come and you'll see," he told her, and, still holding her arm, he led her out of the building.

It was not until they reached the sidewalk that Helia realized what he was talking about. Drawn up to the curb was a vehicle that had once been a Ford. Now it was held together by baling wire and adhesive tape. The left fender was so squashed out of shape that it was a wonder it still remained connected to the body.

For a moment, Helia could only stare. Then Lillemor and Bodil got out of the back seat.

"Isn't it wonderful?" said Bodil. "The boys got a car so that they could take us all home for Thanksgiving."

"That's a car?" said Helia. "I thought it was part of a float for a depression parade." Then she saw the expression on Peter's face, and felt sorry. "I didn't mean it," she said. "But do you honestly think we can make it in that?"

"Make it!" cried Wilhelm and Oivind Otness together as they came around from the other side of the car.

"I'll bet we make just as good time as Professor Winters in his Plymouth, the way he drives," Wilhelm bragged. "We're experts, we want you to know."

"All right, I believe you," Helia said. "It's a great car."

"I'll have you know this car has one of the finest engines ever to come off a Detroit assembly line," Peter told her in the pompous voice of a radio announcer.

This set them all laughing.

"Are we going to get started or spend Thanksgiving here?" Lillemor demanded.

"Wait a minute," Helia said, "while I run up to my room to get a few things."

"Patience, my fair lady," Wilhelm told Lillemor. "We were only waiting for you members of the gentler sex to become fully aware of the qualities of the chariot in which you are to embark on a great adventure."

"I hope there won't be one," said Helia apprehensively.

"Don't worry," Wilhelm assured her. "We are prepared for anything. Glue, all sorts of tools. Besides, I'd trust Peter to get us through anything and anywhere."

As they got started, they were silent, and Helia sat thinking how everyone loved and trusted Peter. He was the most popular boy on campus, even though he had to work so hard that he had little time for social activities. His one good suit was beginning to show its age, and he certainly had very little money to spend on girls. A Coke date was about the best he could manage.

The car ran as well as could be expected for five minutes when, without warning, it stopped.

"And now how is the best engine that ever came off Detroit's assembly line?" came from the back seat.

Peter and Oivind got out.

"Get the shovel," Wilhelm told them. "The dust from the fields and the gravel from the road have piled up like a big mound."

Oivind started shoveling, and before long the six were on their way once more.

From the outset the car had been making considerable noise; now it began to make a grinding sound.

"She's got dust in her lungs," said Peter. "But not enough to choke her."

"I'm glad for every mile we make," said Bodil.

"It will certainly shorten hitchhiking, if that becomes necessary," Lillemor agreed.

The car continued along, and at a fairly rapid pace. Two small villages were passed, and everyone's spirits began to rise.

"Why don't you girls entertain us by singing?" Peter asked. "You ought to be paying for your ride."

Helia started "Over the River and Through the Woods."

"You should sing, 'Over the Ruts and Through the Dust,'" Wilhelm suggested.

"By the way," Helia said, "just how did you acquire this treasure? You were so vague about your plans, I took it for granted you were going to work during Thanksgiving vacation."

"It took a lot of planning, and we didn't say anything because we didn't want to raise any false hopes," Wilhelm told her.

"They didn't tell Lillemor and me anything about it until yesterday noon," Bodil said. "We expected to stay in town."

"Well," Peter said, "it all happened rather suddenly. Wilhelm and Oivind came down to the laundry about a week ago and said they had found a car that was in a wreck. It had been pretty badly damaged."

"I can believe that," said Helia, laughing.

"We could get it for seven dollars. The engine is good, and that's what really matters. So, the three of us paid for the car and got the license. We worked on it whenever we could, and by six o'clock this morning we had it in pretty good condition."

"How did you and Bodil manage to get the time off?" Helia asked.

"I didn't have any trouble," Lillemor said. "Mrs. Little said that if I had a chance to get home she would let me go."

"It was different in my case," Bodil told her. "Mrs. Swift had counted on me to serve and help prepare the Thanksgiving dinner, and I didn't want to leave her in the lurch."

"Well, you certainly didn't," Lillemor said. "You should see everything she did."

"Well, you helped me. We cleaned and stuffed the turkey and let it get a good start in the oven so it will only take about an hour today to finish roasting it. And we prepared everything the way the efficient Swifts have been doing it for years and years. But, thank goodness, I'm going home."

As Bodil told her how they had managed to get away, Helia thought she noticed that the car was wobbling, but perhaps it was only the unevenness of the road.

"I think one of the tires is leaking," said Peter, and stopped the car.

The boys got out to look.

"It's the left front," said Wilhelm. "I was a little afraid of that one from the start."

"Do you have a spare?" Helia asked.

"A spare?" said Wilhelm. "What do you think we're made of—money?"

"Out with the patches," said Peter. "Help me get this thing off, will you, Oivind?"

It took nearly half an hour to get the tire off, and much longer to get it patched.

"I'm getting hungry," Lillemor said. "I was so excited this morning I hardly ate any breakfast."

Helia knew better than to suggest that they stop for sandwiches. Such an extravagance was out of the question. Fortunately, her home would be the first place they reached, and her mother would be sure to take care of them all. They could at least count on plenty of home-made bread and apple butter.

She wondered whether the church would have its Thanksgiving celebration as usual. With conditions as they were, how could they ever manage it?

In the country parish to which Helia's parents belonged, Thanksgiving was a community affair. The celebration lasted all day, and the preparations began months in advance. Helia had helped her mother during the summer to get ready for it. With almost no work to be done in the dust-choked fields, the two of them had made articles for the church. They washed and carded wool that had been stored from last year's shearing, and with cloth they had bought by the bolt from a mail-order house had made warm comforters to be sent to an Eskimo mission in Alaska. They had cut bits of cloth, too small to use in piecing the quilts, and had used them to fill pillow coverings. Helia's mother called them snip pillows. And from old rags they had cut and sewed carpet strips which old Grandmother Knudsen wove on her loom into rag rugs. These rugs would be sent to countries where the church had missions, and would cover dirt floors.

But would there also be the bounteous meal of chicken, mashed potatoes, creamed carrots, mounds of freshly baked bread and buns, apple pie and coffee—the usual menu at the church on such occasions? Probably not, though her mother and the other women of the parish would certainly do their best to provide food for the big dinner. Helia smiled as she remembered how her father used to tease her mother during the orgies of the canning season.

"You remind me of Joseph's interpretation of Pharaoh's dream," he told her, "when the seven fat heads of cattle were raised to be devoured by the seven lean ones."

Well, the lean years were here now, and her mother had certainly done her best to prepare for them.

"If we get home early enough, perhaps we can all go to church," said Helia, breaking a long silence.

"With the coating of dust we're all getting," Bodil said, "I'd be terribly embarrassed to break in on such a gathering."

"Dust is nothing to anyone these days," Wilhelm said.

Again there was silence. Helia wondered what the family might be doing at this very moment. When the church services were over, they usually lingered in the churchyard. Her father had helped to dig the first grave there and put up the first tombstone, which marked the resting place of old Grandfather Ness. Helia remembered how lovely it had been in the years when there was plenty of rainfall. Poplar trees shaded it in many places, and willows grew along the small creek at the bottom of the slope that marked its east boundary. Often the relatives of those lying there planted geraniums that they had carefully tended during the winter months, and later in the season boxes of blooming petunias. But the last time she had visited the churchyard, only the tombstones themselves had withstood the ravages of wind and dust.

Helia was jarred out of her daydreaming by a sudden jolt, and the car stopped.

"We'll have to sit here awhile," Wilhelm said. "The radiator is overheated."

Peter got out and waited a little before he unscrewed the cap. "We'll have to have water to fill her up," he said.

Helia looked about her. All she could see was dusty fields on both sides. Not a house or a tree or anything else.

"The lady is too thirsty to move another inch," said Peter. "Oivind, want to come with me?"

It seemed ages before they returned. But finally Bodil spotted them far up the road, carrying a tin bucket.

"I promised faithfully to return the bucket," Peter said. "It's the only one they have."

At last the car started, but only after it had uttered a few choking complaints.

"The lady really has dust in her lungs," Peter said.

It was not long after that the car began to wobble perilously.

"Another tire gone, I'll bet," came from Oivind.

"The lady's boots *are* a little worn."

Helia seemed to detect a note of anxiety in Peter's voice.

The three boys got out and started to remove the tire. But this time the trouble was more serious and took longer to repair. It was growing dark, too, although it was not late in the afternoon.

"We'll have to turn on the headlights," said Peter, after the tire was on again. "We don't want to risk a collision."

"Not on this road," said Oivind. "But I'll bet we're the only people setting out on such a fool's errand."

"I'll coax her along," Peter said. "I'm sure she won't let us down again."

In spite of the headlights, it was almost impossible to see more than a few feet ahead, and Peter slowed the car down to a crawl. Helia, to keep her mind off her fears, tried to make out the telephone poles along the road and count them. But soon the dust made it too murky to see them. So then she began to count with nothing more in mind than counting.

"I thought you girls were going to give us a concert," Peter said at length.

They began to sing, and after a while the boys joined in.

"I recognize the road now," Helia said. "We're almost home."

"I told you our lady wouldn't disappoint us," Peter gloated. And this time there was genuine relief in his voice.

Finally, there was the slightest glimmer of light a short distance away on the right side of the road.

"That's our house!" Helia exclaimed. "See the shadows up ahead from the evergreen hedge."

Before many more minutes had passed, they had turned up the private road that led to the farmhouse. The engine began a terrific chugging.

"Now, lady," Peter said as soothingly as though he were talking to a child, "you've done beautifully. It will only be minutes until we can give you a rest."

The car came to a halt. And barely visible in the dusty atmosphere, but directly in line with the headlights, Helia made out the figure of her youngest brother, Norman.

"It's Helia!" he called out. "I told Daddy all along you would be home for Thanksgiving."

Sounds of more voices came from the direction of the house, and soon the entire Singstad family surrounded the car.

Helia leaped out and the next instant was hugging and kissing both her parents. Then she turned to her brothers, and for a few moments there was wild confusion, everyone talking at once, and their dog Fido barking vociferously and trying to leap on Helia's shoulders.

"I told you she'd come!" Edvard exclaimed. "All afternoon Fido kept running from one window to another and whining the way he does when he expects someone."

"But who is with you in the car?" asked Helia's father. "They must be tired and hungry."

"Yes," her mother chimed in. "Tell them to come in, and I will get you all something to eat."

There was much shaking of hands and exchanging of greetings, and then they all went to the house, Helia holding tight to her mother's arm.

"Mother, I'm so thrilled, I can scarcely believe it's true that I'm actually here."

As soon as they were inside the house, Helia's mother said, "There's warm water in the stove reservoir, so you can each take turns for a wash in the kitchen."

"I'm sure we need it," Bodil said. "I never swallowed so much dust in my life."

"Well, you didn't get it all," Theodore teased. "Look at Helia."

"I wouldn't care if the dust were an inch thick," said Helia, "and if it took hours to get rid of it. The trip was worth everything it cost." She looked around her home, and it had never seemed so beautiful and welcoming as it did that instant.

Edvard was sent out to the granary for dry corncobs with which to kindle a quick fire, and Theodore went down into the round brick cellar for a jar of apple butter.

"Did the neighbors get together at church?" Helia asked.

"Oh, yes," her mother told her. "But the weather was so bad we left early. We had a different menu this year, baked beans and potato salad, but we enjoyed it as much as anything we had ever had."

"I teased Mother when she insisted we thresh all those beans," said Mr. Singstad, "but as usual she was right." He had been helping Norman with setting the table and bringing chairs.

"We didn't intend to descend on you like this," Peter said, after he had had his turn at the washbasin. "But I guess we were a little too optimistic about our car."

"We're very glad to have you here," said Mr. Singstad, "and we can put you all up for the night."

Soon an inviting fragrance of baked beans and freshly brewed coffee filled the room. "Now you can eat to your heart's content," said Mrs. Singstad, putting a huge plate of potato salad on the table.

"I don't think I was ever so hungry in my life," said Lillemor, when she had finally eaten enough to be able to talk.

After the meal was over, Wilhelm Otness called his parents over the party line. "I guess every family is listening," he laughed, as he heard the clicking as one receiver after another came down.

"Will you tell them to notify my folks?" Lillemor asked.

There was a short silence as Wilhelm held his ear to the receiver. "Your father is on the line," he said finally. "Want to talk to him?"

Lillemor took the receiver. "He says he'll come for all of us tomorrow," she said, "as our chariot would certainly never make it."

After the dishes were washed, with everyone helping, Mrs. Singstad went upstairs to make extra beds on the floor for the three boys. Then everyone gathered in the parlor.

"How are you making out at school?" Mr. Singstad asked.

"All right, I guess," said Wilhelm. "At least, we all have jobs and no one has been asked to leave college so far."

"That's all that matters," Mr. Singstad said. "Get an education, and everything else will come out all right."

Pretty soon Helia found she had all she could do to keep her eyes open.

"I guess you have had quite a Thanksgiving Day,"

Mrs. Singstad said. "So perhaps, Father, we should have our evening devotion, so that the young people can get to bed."

It was the story of the loaves and fishes that Mr. Singstad chose to read. And after he had finished he prayed that, as the Lord was bountiful to His children of old, so they would trust in Him now and not be concerned for their daily bread.

The following morning, shortly after breakfast, Mr. Hegg arrived to pick up the young people. When he saw the car that had brought them to the Singstad farm he couldn't believe his eyes, and said severely, "That thing might have turned turtle on you a hundred times!"

But Wilhelm and Oivind, supported by Peter, insisted that with careful driving it was absolutely safe.

Helia spent the rest of the morning helping her mother sweep up the dust that had seeped into the house during a windstorm the previous night. She had brought some of her books with her, but she didn't have the heart to leave the housework all to her mother. Mrs. Singstad stirred up a batch of dough for potato doughnuts and after many protests agreed to let Helia fry them while she lay down for a nap. To Helia's amazement, Theodore tied a dish-towel around his waist and offered to help.

Helia rolled out the dough and cut it with the doughnut cutter into thick round rings while Theodore stood over the hot kettle of lard, skillfully lifting each puffy brown ring when it was done and tossing it on the drain pan.

"I never knew potatoes could be used in so many ways," he remarked. "We have potato doughnuts, potato pan-cakes, potato bread, potato soup—not to mention all the different ways Mother serves them as a vegetable."

"I don't see where you got them all," said Helia. "Certainly not around here."

"Edvard and I went up with Dad to Minnesota, and we took old Prince and the big wagon. So many of the farmers in western Minnesota were short of help for the potato picking that we got all the work we wanted. We picked on a sharing basis. Edvard was a little slow, but he managed to keep up with Dad and me."

"How long were you gone?"

"Two weeks. We helped harvest carrots and yellow turnips and onions, too. Mother gave away quite a bit of what we brought back to some of the neighbors who couldn't get away."

"Or wouldn't," said Helia.

"Well, I suppose yes, in some cases. It was hard work, I can tell you. Dad has only lately been able to stand up straight, he strained his back so."

They worked in silence for a few minutes, and then Theodore said, "Does Peter Leegaard say anything about his dad?"

Helia looked up. "No. He never mentions him. I don't think he knows where he is. He is going to stay with the Otnesses for the Thanksgiving holidays."

THE EYES that gazed back at Helia were blue, and the expression in them was troubled.

She was looking at her own face in the shining lid of the bread pan she had bought her mother as a Christmas present, and if she hadn't gotten hold of herself she would have burst into tears.

The idea of giving her mother the bread pan had seemed such a splendid one. It was so difficult to reach the dough in the deep rounded crock that Mrs. Singstad had used for years, and there was always the danger that the crock would fall from the stool on which it rested while the dough was being kneaded. Her mother had often spoken of how wonderful it would be to have a bread pan.

To earn the money, Helia had worked Wednesday and Saturday evenings at the five-and-dime store, and when at last the money in her purse tallied with the price tag on the bread pan she had picked out, it seemed almost too good to be true. She had hurried down to the hardware store and bought it. She had been made even happier when the clerk offered her a copy of the latest *Farmer's Almanack*, which was being given away as a Christmas bonus to the customers who spent more than five dollars in the store. The *Almanack* would make a perfect Christmas gift for her father.

For a while the bread pan had seemed to shine like a gleaming jewel as it stood among the books on her study table. When she worked at the table she moved the pan to her bed, being careful that not the slightest fingerprint should mar its lustrous beauty.

And then had come the disillusionment.

It had happened the day Bodil and Lillemor had called to show her the Christmas presents they had bought for their families. They had even less money to spend than Helia because they were working for their room and board and it was hard for them to fit any extra work at all into their schedules. But Lillemor had painted the Littles' porch furniture and Bodil had washed her employer's kitchen walls and they had each been given a bonus to buy their holiday gifts.

First, Lillemor opened a rather small oblong box, with pink cotton to protect the contents.

"Mother wrote that the noises at home were getting almost beyond her endurance," Lillemor explained, "what with all six of my younger brothers and sisters housebound over the weekends because of the dust storms. And there are times she doesn't dare send them to school, because the flying dust is so heavy and so thick she's afraid they won't find their way home. And then the howling wind and the grit beating against the windowpanes add to the bedlam. So I bought her a mouth organ."

"But won't that only make more noise?" Helia asked.

"In a way, yes. But it will be a pleasant noise. I'm giving it to both Mother and Dad, but it's really for the entire family. I'm going to practice 'Yankee Doodle' and 'Row, Row, Row Your Boat' before I leave for home, so that I can get them started right."

Bodil's present was in a flat, square box. As soon as she opened it, the sweet scent of roses was wafted out. And sure enough, lying in a bed of white tissue paper was a large red French rose on a stem with one bright green leaf.

"Here, smell it," Bodil said, holding the box up close to Helia's face.

Helia took a deep breath. It seemed to her that she was inhaling the sweetness of a real rose, although she knew that it was actually made of a smooth fabric.

"It's for Mother, but Dad will enjoy it too. You know that from all our windows at home now there is nothing to be seen but a sea of dust and the dry remains of sow thistles. Dad is so crippled by rheumatism that he doesn't get about at all, and if Mother is going to town she has to get a lift from the neighbors."

"But won't the scent of the rose disappear after a while?" Helia asked.

"Perhaps. But by that time the dust storms may be over and grass growing again, and in the meantime there will be a spot of color and a sweet scent for them to enjoy. And I thought she might like to pin it on her black felt hat on Sundays to cover a spot that has worn rather thin."

Both girls carefully replaced their gifts in the boxes.

"And what are you taking home?" Lillemor asked.

Helia took four red tissue-paper-wrapped packages from the drawer. "I have all these ready," she said. "The hardware store gave me a *Farmer's Almanack* and I'm giving it to Dad. I have underlined the prediction that the drought will end in May. Mr. Fletcher's bank was giving away paper wallets, so I'm taking one for Theodore in case he ever gets rich."

The three girls began to laugh.

"That will be the day," said Lillemor.

"The laundry where Peter Leegaard works gives away pencils as gifts to their patrons, so he got me some for Edvard. And I'm counting on taking one of the little baskets of candy and peanuts we always get at our last meal in the dormitory dining room for Norman."

"And your mother?" Bodil asked.

Up to now, the girls had been so busy showing their presents that they had not noticed the bread pan on the table. Helia turned around and pointed to it. "This is for Mother," she said. "I know she will be pleased. She has been wanting one for so long to replace the clumsy crock she has been using for years."

For a moment there was silence, and then Bodil blurted out, "Oh, how could you, Helia?"

At first Helia could not believe she had really heard Bodil correctly.

Then Lillemor said, "You don't mean to say that you are calling that a Christmas gift?"

"Of course," said Helia. "Why not?"

"When your mother is staying at home with nothing but dusty fields and thistles and hearing nothing but wind and the pounding of sand at the windows?"

"One or two years more of setting bread in the old crock wouldn't matter," said Bodil. "But there is a limit to what people who are stranded out on farms can stand in the way of wind and monotony. Didn't you hear that they had to take away old Mrs. Klingen? She simply couldn't stand it any longer."

"If I had had the money you put into that bread pan, what a Christmas I would have been able to bring home to my folks!" said Lillemor.

After the girls left, Helia sat stunned. For a long time, she didn't move. Why hadn't she had enough imagination to realize what every member of the family was sacrificing for her? As far as her dad and the boys went, the gifts she had managed to wangle from others would help. But for her mother!

If her mother had felt absolutely certain she couldn't get along without a bread pan, she would have used some of the money she had been saving for her trip to Norway. Even in the pleasant days, when there had been rain and things grew, her mother had wanted things that were not concerned with humdrum daily tasks.

From that moment on, the bread pan became an accusing monster that met Helia's eye whenever she entered the room. If there had been a closet, she would have hidden it inside. But the pioneers who had planned the girls' dormitory had not expected them to be affluent enough to need a room for their clothes. Because the wardrobes that had finally been installed were not very large, the monster either had to rest on the table or on the bed if the table was in use.

Well, there was no help for it. She had spent all her money, and it was too late to do anything about it.

Or was it?

Helia got out her purse and let her fingers slide over the

lining. Sure enough, there it was. The silver dollar she had placed there in November soon after she had begun work at the five-and-dime. She had put it there so that she would not be tempted to spend it, as she intended it for her Christmas offering at the church. Although the minister had a regular salary, the Christmas collection was considered an additional payment for his services in the parish, and he had come to expect it. Helia's father had always insisted that the entire family participate in this offering, from the time the youngest child had been able to walk up to the altar.

Now she took out the dollar and let it lie in the palm of her hand. After all, things were different this year. One couldn't set the same standards for giving. Everyone must realize that.

But for that very reason, her father would be sure to be more concerned than ever about the minister's welfare. There would be parishioners who could not contribute anything at all, and the minister had a wife and five small children.

If she gave only a half-dollar now, perhaps she could save enough to give a dollar and a half at Easter, which was when the parish gave another offering to the minister. Half a dollar couldn't possibly break his budget.

Her brother Theodore had a favorite way of making decisions. He tossed a coin. After thinking about it some more, Helia decided that this was as good a way as any to solve the dilemma. Heads she would buy a gift for her mother, tails she would give the dollar to the church.

She gave the coin a good strong toss: it dropped on the bed, and then she stooped over to look. Yes, heads were up.

What would her father think of a daughter who yielded to such worldly impulses? Never mind. She had made her decision and she would stick by it.

She put on her hat and coat. It was getting late, but the stores would be open. She was supposed to be on her way to the last practice of *The Messiah*, which the choir was to sing the following evening. She was one of the soloists, and her whole family was coming down for the event. But at the moment, nothing seemed more important than finding a present for her mother.

Though the ground was bare of snow, the air was damp and chilly. She walked fast, her mind working at top speed. It was not easy to think of something nice that would cost only fifty cents.

What would Marion Fletcher give her mother? Helia wondered. But she supposed that in spite of all the money Marion had to spend, she probably had an equally difficult time making up her mind.

Helia remembered how Mrs. Fletcher had looked at the coronation. She could almost see her brilliant earrings.

That was it. Earrings. They would be most becoming to her mother, whose face was rather thin. More so than the jeweled earrings dangling on each side of Mrs. Fletcher's round face.

Her mother wouldn't even want anything that was expensive, and at the five-and-dime there was a large jewelry counter.

Helia quickened her steps to a run. She couldn't stand the suspense of waiting to find out if there was a pair pretty enough to suit her mother's conservative tastes.

Fortunately, there was no one at the jewelry counter

when Helia arrived, and there was a whole showcase of earrings.

The girl proceeded to take out card after card of earrings. There were black ones, and pale blue, pink, yellow, purple, and red ones.

A pair of imitation emeralds caught Helia's eye. They were exactly the shade of her mother's best dress—a rayon one she had bought two years ago. And they would match the rosette of ribbon with which she had trimmed her black felt hat. But, no, they were far too beautiful.

Helia picked up the card. "These," she asked. "What is the price of them?"

"Sixty-five cents."

She couldn't possibly place thirty-five cents in small change on the altar. Her father would be ashamed of her.

"I—I was thinking of fifty cents," Helia said.

The girl stood silent for a moment. Then she said, "Well, you have worked here, and I know Mr. Franz has been very well satisfied with you. Just wait a moment."

Helia stood holding her breath, and when the girl returned she was all smiles.

"He says it will be all right and for me to give you a gift box, too."

Helia fairly flew to the dormitory. She would have to do without dinner or miss the rehearsals. A bus passed her by, but she couldn't think of wasting money on that, *Messiah* or no *Messiah*.

She was out of breath when she arrived at the chapel, but she had made it on time and, most important, she now had a beautiful present for her mother.

Professor Rimberg was unusually exacting that evening.

It took hours to go through the whole oratorio, and it was midnight when the group was finally dismissed and Helia was back in her room.

As she slipped off her dress, her thoughts went back to the earrings. Were they really as beautiful as they had seemed in the brightly lighted five-and-dime? It would be a pity to unwrap the package, so neatly and attractively done. Yet she simply had to see the earrings once more.

They were even more beautiful than she remembered. And they would be most becoming with her mother's graying blond hair, her fair complexion and delicate features. Helia was very proud of her beautiful mother.

Then suddenly it came to her. Why couldn't her mother wear the earrings when she attended the performance of *The Messiah* tomorrow night?

Yes, she would show the earrings to her mother the very first thing when she arrived. With her green dress and her black hat, even if it was a little threadbare, her mother would look most attractive.

Having come to this decision, Helia undressed and fell asleep at once.

But the minute she awakened the following morning, she knew that something was wrong. Something was making her uncomfortable. Oh, yes. The earrings. What was the motive in giving her mother the earrings before Christmas? Was it to satisfy her own ego so that her mother would look more beautiful sitting in the audience while Helia was singing in *The Messiah*? No wonder such a selfish motive was spoiling all the joy she usually felt at Christmas.

Helia got up, and, still in her nightgown, resolutely

repacked the earrings in their box. When she had wrapped the box again, she felt much relieved.

She looked outside her window and was overjoyed to see that the ground was covered with a light powdering of snow. It would not relieve the parched earth, but it would lay the dust, and it helped to give a sense of the blessed Yuletide season.

Helia gave up trying to study that day; she was too excited waiting for her family to arrive. The gas for the trip to the college and for the drive to the church on Christmas morning would be her father's Christmas gift to the family.

Hour after hour seemed to drag. By three in the afternoon Helia had packed her bag. Finally, supper was over and she began to dress for the concert. She put the bead-spangled band on her hair, even though it would have to be removed later, because she wanted her mother to get the full effect of the lovely outfit she had made for the coronation.

There were only three people at the chapel when Helia arrived, but she knew she would not have long to wait. Her father was never late. And this time Helia was not disappointed. She had scarcely peered from the anteroom where the choir would assemble when she saw her entire family file in.

As she watched them come down the aisle, her heart filled with pride. There was a scrubbed and flawless neatness in their appearance, and it must have taken days to get ready. Theodore had grown an inch this last winter, and her mother must have had to lengthen the sleeves of his coat and the trouser legs of his best suit. The boys' suits and her father's were cleaned and pressed so carefully that they looked like new, threadbare though they really were. As for her mother, in her green dress and black cloth coat, Helia thought she had never seen anyone more beautiful.

She rushed from the anteroom to greet them.

"Oh, I'm so happy you could all come!" she cried, kissing each of them in turn.

Edvard pulled back, his face red with embarrassment. "You don't have to eat me up," he growled.

His father laughed. "Edvard is at the age when any expression of affection embarrasses him, except from Fido."

Edvard ducked his head. But the look on his face reassured Helia that she did not have to worry about Edvard's secret feelings for the human race, even though his expressions of affection at present were lavished only on the dog.

"Is Peter Leegaard going to be here tonight?" Mr. Singstad asked. "Mother thought we might take him home with us."

"He'll be here, all right," Helia said. "But he is spending Christmas with the Otness boys."

At that moment Dr. Winters entered the chapel and made his way up to them.

"This is your family, I take it," he said to Helia. "This must be your mother, but you look enough alike to be sisters."

Helia blushed at the compliment.

She introduced the members of her family, and Mr. Singstad shook hands warmly. "My daughter has told us how you came all the way from the East to teach at our small college."

"It has been refreshing to spend the school year here," Dr. Winters assured him.

"It's too bad you happened to strike this year when there's been so little rain. Otherwise our state really is the garden spot of the United States."

It seemed to Helia that Dr. Winters' face did not register much enthusiasm at this idea.

Her father went on. "I'd like you to come out to our place and see how we farmers live in the West. Say about Eastertime, when there is sure to be some rain and everything will be fresh and green."

This time Dr. Winters did show interest. "I shall take you up on that," he said. "I should like to see more of this country while I'm here."

Helia felt mixed emotions. She wanted to learn more about this elegant professor, whom most of the girls in the class secretly adored. And yet she wondered how he would fit into the farm household, even for a day. Well, Easter was a long way off.

By now the chapel was beginning to fill up, and Helia hurried into the anteroom to get into her choir gown.

If the rehearsal had been disappointing, it bore no resemblance to the performance that night. Never had Helia felt in such an enthusiastic mood or been so much in love with the music; and everyone in the chorus seemed to share her feelings. Professor Rimberg directed with such vigor that he and the singers worked together as one, and when the music ended, the audience was silent for a moment before it broke into the loudest applause ever heard under the chapel roof.

If Helia had ever had any doubts about her family's

pride in her, they were put to an end that night. Her parents openly wept. Theodore patted her shoulder and said, "You were great." Norman reached up to give her a hug, and even Edvard shyly but firmly took her hand.

It was past midnight when they finally reached home. The ride had been chilly, since there was no heater in the car, but her mother had been baking most of the day and the kitchen was snug. And some heat had escaped through the register up into the bedrooms.

Except for Edvard, who went out to see his dog, the whole family went immediately upstairs and to bed. But Helia was too excited to sleep, tired as she was. Finally she did drop off, and the next thing she was aware of was the delicious aroma of food from the kitchen.

When she came downstairs, she noticed that her mother had taken away the oilcloth on the kitchen table and was using instead the red-and-white checked linen tablecloth.

"When the snow fell," her mother told her, "light as it was, we hoped it would settle the dust enough so that we could dress the house up a little, if only for Christmas Day. Fortunately, there is no wind."

It was then that Helia saw the red-and-white checked curtains at the kitchen window. And when she went into the parlor she found that her mother had put back the rag rug on the floor and the best runner on the parlor table, with the blue flower vase and the photographs standing on it. The newspapers which had been covering the upholstered furniture had been removed.

"How wonderful to be really living again!" Helia exclaimed.

"Now come and eat your breakfast," her mother told her, but she smiled at the compliment.

At five in the evening, the church bells down in the village could be heard heralding in the Yuletide season. Soon there would be a dinner with the traditional rice pudding and pork ribs, such as they had enjoyed every Christmas Eve as far back as Helia could remember.

"Can't we have the presents before we eat?" Norman begged.

"Of course not," Edvard told him.

"It's about all I can do to wait, too," Helia confessed.

"Norman has a surprise for us all," their mother said, "but it will wait. Now, let us sit down first, while Father reads the Christmas gospel."

Every year her father read to them the story of the birth of the Christ Child from the Gospel of Luke. She was able to follow him almost word for word, so familiar had the gospel become to her.

Her father put the old family Bible, with its worn pages and binding, down and folded his hands. "We thank Thee, Lord, for Thy great bounty. That our daughter, who is enjoying the wonderful advantage of a fine education, is now at home with us. We ask that Thou wilt make Thy children all over the world as happy and as fortunate as we are in our home together this evening. We are all Thy children. Amen."

Helia had kept her eyes shut, but she could hear how restless Norman was becoming, and when their father finished he gave an audible sigh of relief.

Helia wondered how her mother managed to serve such delicious meals in spite of the hard times. To be sure, there was only a small piece of pork ribs for each of them. But there were mounds of mashed potatoes and plenty of delicious gravy, along with creamed carrots and fresh rye bread. The rice pudding did not have its usual sugar and heavy cream, but it did have extra cinnamon.

"And now isn't it time for the presents?" Norman asked.

"Of course," his mother told him, "and for your surprise, too."

The presents had been placed on the parlor table. No mention had been made of a Christmas tree. Since no one in the village had any extra money, Mr. Lofgren would not risk importing any, and of course no one could commit the unpardonable sin of hewing down a single growing tree in that desolate country.

The family was now seated in the parlor, and the large drip candle, made out of the candle stubs of former years, had been lit. Suddenly Norman jumped to his feet and rushed into the kitchen.

When he returned, he was carrying a large geranium plant. The flowerpot was covered with red paper and tied with a big green paper bow, but its crowning glory was that it actually had a large red geranium blossoming at the top of a long stem.

Norman carefully made his way over to the table that held the packages and set the plant down far enough away from them to avoid an accident.

"You see," his mother said, "we do have a Christmas tree after all. And all because Norman has nursed this plant carefully from early last fall."

"And our tree grew its own decorations this time," Norman said.

Since Norman was the youngest, and his gift had been presented first, it was decided that Edvard should give his present next. They were all thin flat packages wrapped

in paper and tied with red string. The first one was
addressed "To Dad and Mother."

Mrs. Singstad opened it and unfolded the piece of paper
it contained. "Well, I declare," she said. "Edvard has
written a poem to you and me, Father!" And she handed
the paper over to Mr. Singstad.

He read it aloud to them all:

> "Hail to my mother and my dear dad,
> The finest parents anyone ever had."

The poem to Norman read:

> Sometimes our little brother seems to us a pest,
> But he only has faults just like the rest.

Theodore had done some work at their Uncle Albert's
grain elevator in town. Uncle Albert had had to let all his
help go, with no grain coming in during the drought, and
so he asked his nephew to help out. Theodore's poem read:

> We wish you'd give us of your money
> And we'd think you just as sweet as honey.

And for Helia, Edvard had written:

> Someday we'll be as wise as her,
> And then, boy, but won't we purr!

Theodore's presents were presented next, each one in
an envelope. He had given his mother and father a

dollar each in a crisp new green bill, Helia a fifty-cent piece, and each of his brothers a bright new quarter. It must have taken almost every penny Theodore had earned.

When it came time for the family to open the presents she had given them, Helia wished that the wallet she had for Theodore did not have the words *First National Bank of Wheat City, South Dakota* printed on it. But she felt better when her father suggested that this would always be a reminder to Theodore that, no matter how little he earned, the bank would always be ready to help him to riches as long as he cooperated.

She was glad that she had decided on pencils for Edvard. He was the introvert of the family, and it was not always easy to understand him or to know what he liked. The other presents were right too. But Helia's heart beat faster when her mother came to the large package that had her name on it.

It took some time for Mrs. Singstad to get the knots unfastened, for the present was bulky and it had not been easy for Helia to wrap it. And of course her mother always saved every inch of string that came into the house. Finally, after she had wound the string into a ball, she carefully unfolded the wrapping paper.

"Why, it's a real beauty!" she exclaimed, holding up the bread pan so that everyone could see it. "The finest I've ever seen. I'll be thanking you, Helia, once or twice a week for as long as I keep house."

"And I hope that's going to be—well, forever," said Helia. "Now take the lid off and see what's inside it."

In great surprise, her mother did as she was told. "Why, there's a tiny package, Helia! Is there some mistake?"

"Unwrap it and find out," Helia said.

Helia would never forget the expression on her mother's face when she saw the earrings.

"Put them on and see how they look," said her father.

Helia's mother put them on. "I'm going to tell you all a secret," she said. "You'll think me silly and vain, but ever since I was a little girl I wished that someday I would be a fine lady in America and that I would wear earrings."

They all laughed at this. But for both Helia and her mother, behind the laughter was a suggestion of happy tears.

"I THINK if we start with *Beowulf* it will be all right," Helia said. She and Bodil were sitting at the table in Helia's room while Lillemor reclined on the bed.

"I'll settle for the story of the old woman who turned into a woodpecker because she was too stingy to give King Alfred a good-sized cake," said Lillemor. "I think it must have been a pancake."

All three girls laughed.

"If you start your examination like that, I don't think Dr. Winters is going to think much of you," Helia said. "At least add to the story the small item about the *Anglo-Saxon Chronicle*." She began to run through the stack of papers Dr. Winters had given them to help them prepare for the midyear examinations in his course in Early English Literature.

"That isn't going to help me," Lillemor said. "I might as well be asked to count the drops in the Indian River."

Bodil sighed. "If all these authors would only stay put," she said.

"At least you can give Shakespeare credit for being more considerate," Helia said. "He was born and died on the same day and in the same place."

"If you put that on your examination paper you'll be in trouble," said Bodil. "I think there were a few years intervening between the one and the other."

"I wish we didn't have Shakespeare next term," Lillemor said. "But Helia loves to listen to Dr. Winters' voice."

"I still think he reads beautifully," Helia said. "But that doesn't say I always get the meaning of the poetry he is reading. On the other hand, Robert Browning once said that when he wrote a certain poem only he and God understood it and that now only God knew what it meant. Now, let me go over this quickly and don't interrupt me: *Beowulf, The Anglo-Saxon Chronicle, Piers the Plowman, The Pearl, Sir Gawain and the Green Knight, The Canterbury Tales*, and finally Thomas Malory's *Mort d'Arthur*."

Lillemor got up from the bed and came over to the table. "Did you read that, or did you know it by heart?" she asked curiously.

"I have the outline, so I guess it came out of her head," Bodil said.

"Whew! If Dr. Winters uses you as a yardstick, I won't have a chance." Lillemor's voice was almost tearful. "I simply have to pass this course. Kind as the folks are to me where I work, I simply couldn't go through another winter like this one. I hardly have a minute to myself."

"It's just as necessary for me to finish," Bodil said, and her voice showed the same strain. "You just don't know how important it is."

"When I see the easy time some of these students living in town are having!" Lillemor said. "And then they feel sorry for themselves because they couldn't return to college in the East."

"Well, let's go back to work," Bodil said. "I had to do a lot of persuading before Mrs. Swift let me take the time to come over here, and I don't want to waste it."

"Let's go through it once more," said Helia, giving them the outline material she had worked out during the long periods of hard studying she had done ever since her Christmas vacation.

"How about the Arthurian legend?" said Bodil, staring at the papers. "Do we have to know it in detail?"

"I'll tell you what I have decided," Helia said. "Tennyson's *Idylls of the King* gives a pretty good summary of most of the stories. I'll go over them now."

The two girls took notes while Helia recited.

"I think King Arthur was sort of a dope," Lillemor said. "It must have been tiresome to try to live with such a perfect man."

Bodil laughed in spite of being so tired. "Do you know," she said. "Dr. Winters sort of reminds me of King Arthur. I think it would be awfully monotonous to listen to him reciting poetry all the time."

"He doesn't do it all the time, silly," Helia said. "After all, that's what he's hired for."

"Yes, well—give me one of our boys every time."

"Like Wilhelm Otness?" Lillemor teased.

Bodil blushed. "Well, yes. Or Peter Leegaard. Although he's almost too good to be true, too."

Helia interrupted hotly. "If you mean working the washing machines down in the laundry and peddling the wash all over town—"

"Oh, come on, girls," Lillemor interrupted. "We're supposed to be studying."

It was midnight before Helia decided that they were

too tired to get anything more out of her coaching. "One more session, and I think we'll be all right," she said.

"That's what you think," said Lillemor disconsolately, stifling a yawn.

When the day of the midterm examinations came, a high wind was blowing, and as Helia made her way from the dormitory to the Ibsen Administration Building she could feel the grit between her teeth. It was cold and cheerless in the classroom too, which was quite deserted. The time set for the English examination was two o'clock, and the clock on the wall said twenty minutes of. She removed her coat and put it over her shoulders. It would be difficult to write with it on, although she would have been glad of the extra warmth.

Marion Fletcher arrived with two of her Wheat City friends who had been driven over to school in the Fletchers' car. She had on a gray squirrel coat and hat to match, with a wool navy-blue dress underneath. As she came in she was saying to her friends, "It's writing plenty that counts. No prof is going to read every single word that is written on an examination." Helia did not hear what the other two girls said.

One by one the rest of the students came in, and when the long hand of the clock pointed to five minutes before the hour Helia began to feel uneasy. Where was Peter Leegaard? It would be sheer disaster if he missed the examination, since credit for this course was absolutely necessary for his graduation.

It was one minute to two when he arrived, and his disheveled hair and quick breathing showed how he had been hurrying.

At that moment Vernon Hendrickson, the assistant in

the English department, entered the room with a bundle of mimeographed copies of the examination questions.

So Dr. Winters was not conducting the examination himself.

After she had read all the questions, she felt reassured. Perhaps she would not be able to answer the questions as well as Dr. Winters would have her, but at least she could write something. In the seat in front of her Lillemor was staring up in the air, and Bodil was writing slowly.

Marion Fletcher was the first to leave, and she was wearing a broad grin. Peter Leegaard was the next. And after that, one student after another brought his papers up to Vernon Hendrickson's desk. Helia had finished too, but she wanted to wait for Bodil and Lillemor. It was plain to see they were not having an easy time with the examination. Lillemor would never be really happy in a class in English literature, but Bodil was usually a good student.

When they finally finished, Bodil looked so tired that Helia slipped an arm around her.

"Why don't we go down to the dormitory kitchen?" she suggested. "I hear Mother Gunda has made doughnuts, and maybe we can wangle some hot coffee to go with them."

Mother Gunda had just arrived to start preparations for dinner. The coffeepot was on the coal stove, and the huge pans were piled high with golden rings.

"Sure," Mother Gunda told them. "I was just going to have a snack myself."

The girls each had two cups of steaming coffee and three delicious doughnuts.

"Now that you're more rested," Helia said, "come up to my room and we'll talk over the examination."

When they arrived in Helia's room it was clear that Bodil was completely tired out.

"Why don't you lie down on my bed," Helia suggested, "and listen to what Lillemor and I say? I'll cover you with the wool shawl Mother gave me when I went home for the Christmas holidays."

But the two had scarcely started on the first question when the even breathing from the bed told them that Bodil was fast asleep.

"I don't see how Bodil can keep going if she continues to work so hard," Helia said. "How do *you* manage it?"

"I'm not as conscientious as she is," Lillemor said, "and the household is entirely different. I don't worry so much, either. The drought and the depression have just about cleaned out my folks too. But they are younger than Bodil's, and if we can only get some crops in next year my dad says things won't be too bad."

After the two girls had left, Helia sat wondering what she ought to do. She might have known last fall, when she heard that Bodil was going to be held accountable for every moment of her working day, that sooner or later she would crack. If Lillemor had had the bad luck to be working for such a driver, she'd simply let things go when they got too much for her. Lillemor had started out with the children in the house on her neck, so that she couldn't find time for study. But in her good-natured way she soon put a stop to that without offending anybody. But Bodil was different. She would keep going until she dropped.

Finally Helia made up her mind. She would go to the Dean. She was a little afraid of Dean Estvold but this was important—she had to speak to her.

As soon as she made her decision, she set about at once

putting it into action. She hurriedly brushed her hair, saw that her slip wasn't showing, and then made her way to the Dean's office. Fortunately, she was alone.

As briefly as she could, Helia explained the situation. "Bodil showed me the schedule Mrs. Swift made out for her at the beginning of the semester," she said. "Just doing all that work would be enough of a load to carry, let alone trying to get through all her courses at college."

"Have you spoken to Bodil's parents about the matter?"

"Bodil would never even hint to them that she is being overworked. Her father is so crippled with rheumatism that it is almost impossible for him to move around the place at all, and her mother is even smaller and more fragile than Bodil is."

"I suppose it will mean a great deal to Bodil to finish this year, rather than putting it off until later?"

"Well, what with the drought and the depression, no one is having a very easy time of it these days. And if Bodil could get out and earn money next year by teaching school—well, you understand."

"I do," said the Dean.

Helia rose to go. "I hope you don't mind that I took up your time coming down here. But it was no use talking to Bodil myself."

"I'm very grateful to you," the Dean assured her, and she rose from her chair behind the desk. "We want our girls to give satisfaction where they are employed. But there is a considerable difference between doing one's duty and being imposed on." She smiled. "I will attend to the matter at once."

She came forward and held out her hand. Helia took it,

and went away marveling that the Dean was really such a nice person.

For a few days afterward, she found herself worrying about Bodil's grades in the examination. But there had been no note in her post-office box, so Helia knew she must have had passing grades. And Bodil told her with great surprise that Mrs. Swift had suddenly changed her entire schedule. "I couldn't ask for better conditions than I have now."

As for herself, Helia was sure she had done quite well in her English examination. It came, therefore, as a distinct shock when she found a note in her post-office box saying that Dr. Winters wished to speak to her in his office after class the following day.

Helia grew frightened. She had heard nothing about how she had made out in the English exam, and although she thought she had answered the questions fairly well, she could never be sure. Dr. Winters demanded a great deal of his students, and in spite of the hard work she had put into the course she could not expect to make up for her inadequate background in one semester.

Helia had never been in Dr. Winters' office before and had not expected to see such a change in the familiar room. There were Venetian blinds covering the one large window, so that most of the light came from a softly shaded lamp on the desk. The walls, which she remembered as having been dark, were now a soft green to match the curtains. The whole place was like a breath of spring.

"It's beautiful," Helia breathed.

"You like the change in the room?" Dr. Winters said. "I'm glad of that. The two prints of Westminster Abbey and St. James Cathedral I brought from home, and my mother gave me the rug and the lamp. The college painted the walls, and I bought the Venetian blinds here in town. But I did not call you here to display my office," said Dr. Winters. "It was about your examination that I wanted to speak."

Here it comes, thought Helia, her heart beginning to beat faster.

"I must say I was surprised by it," said Dr. Winters. "I will admit that I had my doubts about the Early English Literature class last fall. The library facilities here are hopeless, and I had a fairly good idea what I might expect from the students."

If I've failed this course, thought Helia, I won't graduate this year. If I thought it would help at this late date, I'd pray.

"Of course," Dr. Winters went on, "in the case of a few students things were different. Marion Fletcher and some other students transferred from institutions that had excellent libraries."

Helia sat motionless.

"But of forty-four students in the class you submitted the outstanding paper."

The words were so unexpected that for a moment Helia could not take them in.

"Every question was answered accurately and to the point. Moreover, the essay questions revealed an insight that would have done credit to a student with access to our best libraries."

Helia could only sit and stare in wonder. Surely she wasn't hearing correctly!

"Either you have a phenomenal memory, or you have applied yourself more vigorously than I would have thought so young and inexperienced a person could."

It was really true then. Dr. Winters was telling her she had written a good examination paper. He was pleased with her. He was actually praising her. It was all so amazing that she could not find words to express her reactions.

"Thank you," she managed to say, and rose to her feet. She did not feel she should take up any more of the professor's time.

Dr. Winters rose too and walked her to the door.

"If this is an indication of what you are really capable of doing, you should go far," he said.

"Thank you," Helia managed to say again, and left the office walking on air.

Praise she was used to. All through the grades she had brought home nearly perfect report cards; she had been valedictorian of her class in high school, and the professors at Nidaros College had approved of her work. But all her instructors, up to now, had grown up in the Dakotas or had come directly from Norway. And she had not had too much competition from her fellow students.

But praise from Dr. Winters was something else again. He had traveled widely and held a doctorate from a fine eastern university.

She, Helia Marie Singstad, had never been outside South Dakota. Her mother had been an emigrant from Norway and her father the son of emigrants. She loved and honored them, but they had no book learning, except for the Bible and church hymns. There had never been the time or opportunity for anything else. It was because they had been deprived of formal education that they were making such a sacrifice for her.

But to have her work praised by Dr. Winters, who seemed to Helia an intellectual giant—well, that was almost beyond her fondest dreams.

She had registered for Dr. Winters' course in Shakespeare for the second semester, and now she could scarcely wait for the first class.

HELIA arrived early on the first day of her Shakespeare
class and took a seat near the window. It was slightly open,
for the day was unusually warm for February. It seemed
ages since the weather had been mild enough to be out-
of-doors at all.

To her surprise, Marion Fletcher came and sat beside
her.

"I hear that you rate with Dr. Winters," Marion said.
Helia looked at her in surprise.

"Dr. Winters told my father he'd never been so surprised in his life as when he read your examination paper.
You see, my father is simply daft on education. And when
he heard how well you'd done, and I barely came through
with a C in the course, there was the deuce to pay."

"He's a good teacher," Helia managed to say.

"That's what Dad thinks. He wants to know why I
haven't learned more on my trips abroad. But I went with
Mother, and the hotel accommodations are all that matter
to her."

By this time the room was filling up. Then the bell rang,
and the hubbub of conversation stopped suddenly as
Dr. Winters entered.

He went up to his desk on the slightly raised platform, glanced at the open window, and frowned.

"Please close that window, Mr. Leegaard," he said. "I don't wish to inhale any more of this South Dakota dust than is absolutely necessary."

For a moment, Helia was so disturbed that she felt she must apologize for the drought. But Peter's face was expressionless as he closed the window.

Dr. Winters sat down and started to call the roll, but it was a few minutes before the frown left his handsome face.

"I take it," he said, "that most of you already own a complete set of the works of Shakespeare. But in case there should be a few exceptions, I shall have all those in the college library put on reserve."

Helia had a sinking feeling. A complete set of Shakespeare! At home there was the family Bible and the hymn books that she and Theodore had each been given for confirmation. And her mother had brought over with her some stories by Björnstjerne Björnson. All the other books she had read had come from their school library or from Nidaros College.

"To begin with," Dr. Winters continued, "we shall discuss the two long poems, *Venus and Adonis* and *The Rape of Lucrece*." He asked if anyone had any questions, but as no one seemed to have any, he gave them a brief account of Shakespeare's life, and dismissed them.

Bodil and Lillemor waited outside for Helia.

"I can't imagine how we're going to get to the library to work," said Lillemor.

"I thought of one thing we might do," Helia suggested.

"Go downtown to the public library and try to take out copies of Shakespeare's works in one volume, and if there's only one copy we could share it."

Marion Fletcher must have overheard the conversation, for she came up to them. "There are any number of volumes of the complete works of Shakespeare at the Masonic Library," she said. "It seems they were willed by members who have passed on, and no one ever looks at them. My father belongs to the local chapter, and I think he would get a copy for each of you."

It just goes to show, Helia thought, that you can never know where you might receive help. Marion Fletcher was the last person to whom she would have turned for anything.

On the following Sunday, Helia, Bodil and Lillemor went for a long walk to get away from their books for a while. They asked Peter and the Otness brothers to go with them, and it was three o'clock when they assembled in the north parlor of the dormitory.

"I wonder how the weather will turn out," Bodil said. "Lillemor and I were almost blown away when we climbed the hill up to the campus."

"Well, let's get started," Helia said. "If it's too bad we can always turn back."

Peter opened the door leading out on the porch of the dormitory. The wind was raging with such violence that he hurried to shut it again.

"That may be only a gust," Helia said hopefully.

"All right," said Peter, "but it felt more like a storm to me."

The six battled their way to the edge of the campus.

"I'm beaten," Helia admitted. "Let's turn back."

"Where shall we go?" Bodil asked. "There's always such a crowd in the parlors of the dormitory—especially in weather like this."

"Let's try the door into the gymnasium," suggested Wilhelm. "If it's open we might sit in there."

To everyone's relief the gymnasium was open. The boys brought chairs into a circle in one corner of the main room. It was quiet there, and a relief to be out of the wind and the clouds of dust.

"I suppose we oughtn't to be talking shop," said Oivind, "but I'm worried about this Shakespeare course."

"So am I," said Lillemor. "I thought we were going to study the plays. But all we've had so far is poems, and I can't make head or tail of them."

"That's because you don't have the poetic spirit," Wilhelm teased.

"I certainly wish he would do something besides read passages from Shakespeare's poems and talk about their structure."

"Dr. Winters wants us to have a thorough grounding before we go any further," Helia said, but she had to admit that she, too, was disappointed. She could not remember anything about the two long poems. And as for the sonnets, if she was honest with herself she had to admit that she found them very difficult.

"I think the trouble is," Bodil said, "that we are not really capable of appreciating either Shakespeare or Dr. Winters. It reminds me of the story of William Lyons Phelps. He paid several hard-earned dollars to go to a concert, and came away disappointed. So he went to the head of the music department and said, 'I want you to help me so that next time when I go to a concert I'll get my money's worth.'"

"Well, don't you think that is exactly what Dr. Winters' job is supposed to be?" asked Peter mildly.

"He reads beautifully," Helia said.

"You are simply carried away by his manner," said Wilhelm. He rose to his feet and started letting his voice rise and fall dramatically: "The weather is abominable. If this drought does not stop soon, we shall all be buried alive in the dust. And a thousand years from now, when the archaeologists are excavating among the ruins, they will find us all in the dust of Nidaros College."

The imitation was so perfect that they all burst out laughing.

"All I say," said Helia, feeling ashamed after their laughter was over, "is that the trouble isn't Dr. Winters' or Shakespeare's. We'll just have to concentrate and put our minds on what we're doing. Shakespeare wouldn't still be read if he weren't a giant of literature, and if people did not enjoy reading him, and Dr. Winters is a scholar. So I suggest we all stop feeling sorry for ourselves and try to appreciate what we are getting."

In the following weeks she listened carefully while Dr. Winters explained about the history plays and while he read long passages to the class. It was not easy to keep the Richards and the Henrys apart, and she was relieved when they moved on to *Julius Caesar.*

She was early to class one day, and Peter caught up with her in the hall. "Why so early? We have twenty minutes yet."

"I finished at the library," said Helia, "and it was too late to go back to the dormitory."

"Same thing. Not the library. Business for White's Laundry. Want to ride on my handlebars?"

They laughed, and walked into the still empty classroom.

"By the way, Helia, how do you think you fared in the examination on what we have done so far?"

Helia hesitated. "All right, I hope." But she realized that her manner did not match her words.

"So? I expect we answered the same way, like parrots. But honestly, Helia, I wish it were like a problem in chemistry where you could look at the evidence and come to a definite conclusion."

"I don't know if I answered the question about the structure of *Julius Caesar* correctly. The first act giving the setting—the return of Caesar and his being offered the crown, and so on—the second act the conflict, the third the climax, and so on. I have a feeling if I ever get to teaching Shakespeare to my English students, I'm going to make a mess of it."

"I wonder," said Peter, "if Shakespeare wrote it with all these things in mind. Dr. Winters makes it sound as though he had been putting on a puppet show, and setting up Julius and the rest like so many dummies."

Helia sighed. "I wish I were a better student, so I could follow Dr. Winters better."

"I wish he'd come down to earth," said Peter, "so we could all follow him."

It both surprised and amused Helia to hear Peter express himself so strongly. The Shakespeare class was at least doing that for him.

"This week," said Dr. Winters, after he had called the roll, "we are going to try something new."

He explained that the students were to divide in small groups, each selecting one of the plays they had not read in class on which to report. They would discuss their reactions among themselves, choose suitable quotations, and then report to the rest of the class. "I took part in a program like this when I was a student. We all found it both helpful and enjoyable." He then called for volunteers, since each group would be headed by a captain.

After a moment's silence, Marion Fletcher said she would be willing to head one group, and she chose several of her friends from Wheat City to work with her.

To Helia's amazement, Bodil offered to head another, if Lillemor would act as captain along with her. They chose Oivind Otness and two students from the town to join them.

Helia sat wondering what she should do. English was her major, and it was up to her to get as much out of the class as possible. But she was afraid she would not do a good job and she felt self-conscious about volunteering.

"Why don't you say you'll be captain?" Peter whispered to her. "I'll help you."

He *has* changed, thought Helia. And then Wilhelm Otness offered to help, too.

After class was dismissed she asked Bodil, "How did you ever muster up enough courage to volunteer?"

"I knew I'd have to be in one group, and as Lillemor lives close to me it would be easier if we did things together. Oivind and the others say they will arrange their time to suit ours."

"We've talked to Marion," Bodil went on. "She's going

to telephone us so we won't choose the same play she does."

"When you've heard from her will you let me know? Then we can work out our plans too."

At nine o'clock that night, Bodil called to say that Marion's group had selected *The Merchant of Venice* and that she and Lillemor were going to do *Macbeth*.

Helia sat up half the night going over the plays, and finally decided to suggest to Peter and Wilhelm that they report on *A Midsummer Night's Dream*. She thought the class might enjoy one of the lighter plays, and moreover, she was familiar with Mendelssohn's musical setting to the play, and loved it. Tomorrow, when she met Peter, she would ask him what he thought of her choice. After all, if he and Wilhelm had another choice, she could not consider reporting on it.

The best dramatic parts for the boys would be the play the artisans perform in honor of the Duke's wedding. They were comical parts, and she knew Peter and Wilhelm would like them, and if she were needed she could take a minor role.

What she wanted to tell the class, however, was what the play meant to her and how it reminded her of their farm. When she thought of her home, it was of the years when there had been green fields and luscious fruits and flowers to gather.

And she could make her presentation much more beautiful with the addition of real music. At first she hesitated about suggesting this since they would have to go outside their class for the performers. But she knew that Sylvia Lindstrom and Martin Moss would be glad to come and play Mendelssohn's music on their violins with Henry Nyvold on the flute. All of them belonged to the college symphony orchestra and were excellent players.

At first the boys objected to her idea. Peter said he wasn't an actor.

"Well, is there anything to prevent your becoming one, at least for the occasion?" asked Helia. "After all, it can't be any worse for you than it is for me to struggle over chemistry formulas."

"There's nothing to them," protested Peter.

"Nor to becoming Peter Quince instead of Peter Leegaard," Helia said, and laughed.

When Wilhelm read Bottom's lines he was most enthusiastic. "He's a screwball," he said, "and I'll have a lot of fun acting him."

Wilhelm never ceased to surprise Helia. This year he had changed more than anyone else she knew on the campus.

They arranged for two practice sessions before the day they were to perform. And although they were convulsed with laughter, especially at Wilhelm's interpretation of Bottom's part, they managed to have the selection fairly well in hand when they had finished their practicing.

When the great day arrived, there was an air of suppressed excitement in the classroom. Those who were giving reports occupied the front seats, and the rest of the class sat farther back.

As soon as the bell had rung, Marion rose and took her place just in front of the raised platform. She was dressed in a simple but elegant wool dress, with a chain of black and gold beads around her neck. Helia thought she made a picture that any girl would be proud and happy to see confronting her in the mirror. Even her gunmetal stockings and her modish pumps were in the height of fashion.

"I chose to report on *The Merchant of Venice*," Marion began, and went on to explain that because the medieval church forbade usury, the Jews had done all the lending of money before formal banks were established. People had not yet realized that it was only fair to pay interest for the privilege of borrowing money; after all, the lender should be paid for the risk he takes. Because of this lack of understanding, the Jews were often despised and even persecuted.

"Bassanio, the young lover, really had no business wanting to borrow all that money. Of course," Marion went on, "it was wrong of Shylock to demand a pound of flesh as a penalty for failing to make good the payment at the required time. But he had been driven to great anger and had been humiliated by the constant reviling of those who borrowed money from him."

Helia marveled at the ease and composure with which Marion spoke. She hoped she could do even half as well when her turn came.

At this point Marion announced that her group would now read a portion of the scene in which the bond was posted.

"Then," she said, "comes the famous trial scene. Many people think that Shylock is an ogre here. But he has many successors, my father says, in our day, when unscrupulous loan companies prey upon those desperate enough or careless enough not to check what they have been agreeing to. And here we'll present the section where Shylock demands his pound of flesh.

"There is one final point I would like to bring out," Marion said, "and that is Shakespeare's sense of humor. He certainly put those two young men on the spot, when Nerissa and Portia demand to know what became of the rings they had sworn not to part with till their dying day."

There was a ripple of laughter through the classroom, and Helia knew that Marion was scoring with the rest of the students. She herself had sat spellbound during the presentation.

"Oh, yes, I forgot. There is one other detail which I thought was very significant," Marion added. "Less than a dozen years ago American men did not consider women bright enough to vote. Yet Shakespeare, well over three hundred years ago, entrusted the laws of the court to his heroine Portia."

As Marion took her seat there was a burst of applause and there were smiles of approval on all the students' faces.

Bodil got up next, and Helia could not help worrying about her. What chance would this simple farm girl have to make a favorable impression, coming right after Marion Fletcher?

Bodil's small oval face wore an expression of tense and anxious concentration. Her blue sweater and gray wool skirt had already given much service, and she was wearing what Helia knew was her only pair of good stockings. Her parents were honest, hardworking, and not at all ignorant, but they could not begin to give Bodil the things Marion's parents had showered on her.

"I chose to report on *Macbeth*," Bodil began, "or rather Lillemor Hegg and I chose to report on it, because after we had read the play and talked it over we felt we had so much in common with Lady Macbeth."

To say that Helia was startled was to put it mildly. But Bodil went on talking carefully and clearly, as though she had been doing public speaking all her life.

"Lady Macbeth," she told her audience, "was unfortunate enough to be living in an era of history where the only hope a woman had to rise from the position in which she had been born was to marry a man who could take her along with him. If he had not yet arrived at the station in life which she wanted him to have, she had only very limited means of assisting him to get there."

It was the prophecy of the witches, Bodil said, which had given Lady Macbeth the idea of helping her husband to become king of Scotland. "I should like the class to hear that prophecy," Bodil said, "and so Oivind Otness will now read it."

Oivind could not by the greatest exaggeration be classed as a fluent reader, but he managed to get through the passage successfully. Then Bodil went on to tell the rest of the story.

"Lady Macbeth must have felt both revulsion and guilt as one murder after another had to be performed. She had both a conscience and a high standard of morals. But senseless ambition, with no legitimate means of attaining it, had deprived her of her real sense of values in life."

Bodil said they would now do the sleepwalking scene, and Lillemor came forward. Her delivery was rather carefree, but as Helia watched she could believe that Lady Macbeth was a real person.

"And now," said Bodil, "I am sure you understand why Lillemor and I chose to report on *Macbeth*. If we had lived back in those days, we might have had to do evil things to get what we wanted, but now we live in an age when any woman, married or unmarried, can get whatever she sets her heart on. Last summer, I wondered whether it was right for me to attend college this year, with things so bad at home. So I asked our minister, and he said that neither a depression nor a drought had ever closed any of our churches here in America. Nor would they close the schools. He said if I really wanted to continue my education I would find a way."

If Helia had been impressed with the applause which Marion had received, she was absolutely thrilled by the thunderous handclapping that greeted Bodil's closing remarks.

Now it was Helia's turn, and she made her way to the front of the class.

If I stop thinking of myself and concentrate on what I'm doing, she thought, I'll get along better. She had dressed very carefully in her best navy wool, because if she did not have to worry about how she looked she could put all her energy into what she intended to say.

"In *A Midsummer Night's Dream*," Helia said, " a great poet was putting into words his love for his surroundings at Stratford-on-Avon. He must have wandered often in the Forest of Arden, both by sunshine and by moonlight." She said she and her brothers had sometimes taken midnight strolls by the brook that skirted the boundary on one side of their place. In summer, there was the continuous mingling of sounds from crickets, frogs, and other live things that could be heard in the night. And when the plum and apple trees were in bloom in the orchard close to the house, it had seemed to her when she was a little girl that a fairy wedding was being staged there.

At this point Helia paused while Peter read, "I know a bank where the wild thyme grows."

Then Helia spoke of Mendelssohn's music, and explained how it fitted into the play.

"And since, according to the scholars, music played such an important part in the presentation of plays in Shakespeare's day, we have taken the liberty of calling on a group of musicians to perform for the class."

The musicians played well, and the class was delighted with this unexpected pleasure.

And now, said Helia, she and Peter and Wilhelm would like to present a dramatic reading from the play, and in making the choice they thought they would use something out of their own experience. They had all attended country grammar schools, and on many occasions the teachers had put on plays in the one-room schoolhouses. Everyone remembered the arguments during rehearsals and the troubles some of the actors got into, and so they would show how a group of mechanics tried to put on a play in honor of the wedding of Duke Theseus and the Queen of the Amazons.

The classroom rang with laughter at Wilhelm playing Bottom and Peter playing Peter Quince. Helia had only a minor part, but when it was over she was drenched in perspiration. She hoped that Dr. Winters would not disapprove of them too much.

When the applause had finally died away, everyone looked at him. He had been sitting in the back of the room, saying nothing.

"I must admit," he said finally, "that those are the three most original presentations of excerpts from Shakespeare's plays that I have ever witnessed. And I have been present at a great many."

He resumed his position at his desk.

"The choice of plays was good, and time and thought have clearly been spent in their preparation. However, the class must not forget that we are dealing here with some of the greatest writing the world has ever seen. You must not try to downgrade them to the level of a pioneer state. We shall now proceed to analyze the structure of each of these three plays."

Helia began to take notes obediently. But she had begun to feel a great deal of sympathy for Shylock and Lady Macbeth, and she also decided that when she had pupils of her own and was presenting *A Midsummer Night's Dream* she would tell them about the fruit trees covered with blossoms in their orchard on a moonlit night in spring.

HELIA sat looking at the printed form in front of her. It seemed hardly possible that she had reached the point of actually applying for a teaching position. That great milestone had once seemed so far away, and now, in only three months, she would be leaving Nidaros College forever. The thought was rather saddening, but the excitement of starting out on a new career was going to be wonderful.

Well, she had better get started.

Name? That was easy. There was only one answer for that—Helia Marie Singstad.

Date of birth? That was easy too. June 5, 1910.

Parents? Andrew Karl and Helena Sanden Singstad.

The subjects she would teach? She would have to think about that a little. She was glad she had taken Professor Gortvedt's advice about being prepared to teach chemistry, although she hoped she would never actually have to do it. Working side by side with Peter Leegaard was one thing, but organizing a class and being responsible for it was something else. Anyway, it looked good on paper, so she put down that she could teach chemistry.

Her music ought to help. She had studied voice for three years and had sung in the choir ever since she had entered Nidaros College.

There wasn't much more she could add, when she had listed her regular major and minors. She had not worked away from home, or traveled, but had spent all four winters in Wheat City and summers at home on the farm.

She filled out the form to the best of her ability and brought it down to the office of the appointment committee. Then she went to her room to meet Bodil and Lillemor, who had also been filling out application blanks.

"I'm hoping the local school board will give me a job for next year," said Bodil. "It would solve most, if not all, of my problems, because I could live at home and contribute some money to the upkeep of the place."

"My father says he's sure you'll be elected," said Helia. "He's already spoken to several of the members."

"I know. Your father is always so kind to everybody."

"I'd like to look into a crystal ball and know where I'll be," Helia said. "I'm going to get a position somewhere if I have to chloroform all the board members. And even if it's out on the Indian Reservation."

"Well, anyway," said Lillemor, "we managed to survive this year. If you both could have just one wish, apart from getting a job and having the drought end, what would it be?"

"I know what I'd wish," said Bodil without the slightest hesitation. "I'd like to check into a good hotel in a large city and settle down in its most luxurious suite and have room service and everything I wanted."

"That sounds like a honeymoon with a millionaire," said

Lillemor. "Me, I'd like to go on a shopping spree and buy outfits for every possible occasion. And before I started I'd get rid of every rag I own, except for just enough to cover me until I could start shopping."

"I'll bet your sisters would appreciate that too," said Helia. "You told me once that your youngest sister has never worn a piece of clothing that hasn't been handed down three or four times."

"That's true," said Lillemor. "Poor Betty. Well, if I had all that money, I would give each of my sisters at least one new outfit, and let them choose it themselves."

"And you, Helia, what kind of a wild spree would you go on?"

Helia closed her eyes. "I'd like to marry someone I love more than anyone else in the world."

"That's no real wish," said Bodil. "Every girl wishes that."

"Helia talks as though she's in love right now," Lillemor said.

"I am," said Helia. "With living. I'm so curious to know what's going to happen tomorrow and next week and next year that I can hardly wait."

Bodil rose to go. "Well, if I don't go and start getting dinner I won't have much to look forward to in the next few hours. It's mashed potatoes and creamed onions and hamburgers tonight, so I'd better get started peeling potatoes."

"Poor Bodil," said Lillemor, after she had gone. "It's too bad she happened to get that particular job. She's so conscientious everyone takes advantage of her."

"Well, it will soon be over," said Helia. "If she gets a

teaching job in her home town, things will be much easier for her next year."

"Yes, that's true. But I hope she doesn't settle down in it for life. Bodil deserves better things."

And so do you, Helia thought. Lillemor was so kind and had such a sunny temper that the man she married would be fortunate.

March was almost over when Helia finally received a note in her post-office box to report to the secretary of the appointment committee. Helia rushed there at once.

"There's a call from Hawk Ridge," the secretary said. "The town has never had a full four-year high school up to now, but they have a new school superintendent, and they are now planning to offer enough courses to give diplomas. Since the high school is not accredited, the fact that we haven't been admitted yet into the North Central Association wouldn't be a strike against us. It would be a particularly good opening for one of our graduates."

Helia was elated. "How far is Hawk Ridge from Wheat City?"

The secretary checked it on the map. "About three hundred miles."

Helia felt her heart sinking. That was a long way to go to apply for a job, but they had insisted that they had to meet the applicant. She thanked the secretary, took the slip, and said she would let her know in the morning what she decided.

When she inquired at the bus station, she found that the connections for Hawk Ridge were very bad. She would have to go far north to Glasgow Prairie and stay overnight, and then take a bus from there to her destination. Apart from her hotel expenses and the food, the bus ticket would cost ten dollars and thirty-five cents.

Back in her room, Helia now added up her resources. She had deposited with the Dean five dollars in a single bill for the rental of her cap and gown. This was the last of the money her mother had saved up for the trip to Norway. Then there was the fifty cents her brother Theodore had given her for Christmas. She had put it in her Bible at the beginning of the Book of Psalms. Finally there were the two dollars and seventy-five cents she had for emergencies. She kept this money in a small coin purse that she pinned with a stout safety pin to her slip.

Eight dollars and twenty-five cents—this was the grand total of her assets. It meant that trying to get to Hawk Ridge by bus was out of the question.

Helia thought of asking Peter Leegaard to help her. But she knew that the rickety old Ford could not go even twenty miles without breaking down, much less three hundred.

The job in Hawk Ridge now seemed the most important thing in the world. She had two strikes against her—no previous teaching experience and the fact that Nidaros College was not accredited. She might never be offered another teaching position.

After history class, Helia told Bodil and Lillemor her problem.

"Hawk Ridge," said Lillemor. "That's where Netta Mellum comes from. The connections are so bad she didn't even get home for Christmas. She's been awfully home-sick because it's her first year and she's never been away from home before. Why don't I ask Netta about her town? I got to know her through the girl that sits next to me in the Shakespeare class."

Late that afternoon, as Helia was on her way to the library, she heard Lillemor calling her.

"I have news for you," she said excitedly. "I got in touch with my friend, and she was able to locate Netta Mellum. She stays at a private house two blocks off the campus. Netta was interested at once. She knows someone named Sadie Hunter, who is a distant relative of her landlady's. And her landlady thought perhaps Sadie Hunter would be willing to take you, if you paid for the gas and oil."

Promptly Helia arranged to meet Sadie Hunter at the house where Netta roomed, and at the appointed time Helia presented herself at the door. Sadie was sitting on the black horsehair sofa, and Helia lost all hope when she looked at her. Sadie was an enormously fat woman in a shapeless wool dress that all but extended to her swollen ankles and oversized feet that were encased in shabby calfskin shoes. If her car and driving matched her general makeup, Helia doubted if they would ever get to Hawk Ridge.

"I'd enjoy getting out for a ride," Sadie said. As she spoke she smiled. Her smile was so warm and sincere that Helia felt much better.

"Have you any idea how much it would cost for you to take us to Hawk Ridge?" Helia asked, sitting down beside Sadie on the sofa. Netta Mellum, a little blond girl, hovered close by.

"Well, let me see," said Sadie, closing her small gray eyes. "We can get five gallons of gas for a dollar."

"And it's three hundred miles to Hawk Ridge?"

"Two hundred and sixty," said Netta. "When my family brought me down last fall, we came the shortest way."

"Let's see," Helia counted. "How many miles to a gallon?"

"We used to get twenty-two on our Ford," Netta put in.

"I have a ten-year-old Dodge—it uses up more gas than that. And then there's the oil, too. Sometimes it feeds heavy—the car, I mean."

They finally decided that six dollars and a half should take care of the gas and oil. That was a big chunk out of her precious eight dollars and twenty-five cents. Netta didn't have any money to contribute. Mother Gunda would put up sandwiches for them, so they would not have to spend anything on food.

It was agreed that they would start out at seven-thirty on Saturday morning. Sadie Hunter made only one stipulation, and that was that she must be home by suppertime on Sunday. Nothing whatever must interfere with that. Helia agreed immediately, for she wanted to be in Hawk Ridge only long enough to have her interview with the school board.

At seven-thirty sharp, Helia was standing on the front steps of the dormitory when Sadie and Netta drove up in the Dodge. Helia regarded the driver with mixed feelings. Her brown wide-brimmed hat was askew and her red coat was clearly in need of both cleaning and pressing. As for the car, it was difficult to say what its original color must have been, since caked and hardened mud covered all its exterior. Still, here was a vehicle on wheels that would take her where she wanted to go, with a chauffeur who seemed capable of driving there.

"I was a little afraid I wouldn't have enough gas to make it here," Sadie said as Helia climbed into the back seat. Netta, at Sadie's request, was occupying the seat next to the driver, in case there was any uncertainty about which road they should take.

"I suppose we had better start at the gas station, then," said Helia. A choking from the engine indicated that something more than gas was needed.

Fortunately nothing happened until the gas station was reached. "Fill her up," said Sadie. "And oil, too. This lady will pay for it."

When the car got started again, it moved right along, and Sadie managed to drive it at an even speed.

Once they had left the paved streets of the city and were out on the dirt road that led into the country, Sadie managed to hit every bump in the road. It almost seemed that she had a peculiar aptitude for striking them at exactly the angle that would most jar the car. Then she would look at the girls with a broad, good-natured smile upon her face.

Helia, alone in the back seat, would not have minded the bumps so much, except that at each jerk a cloud of dust rose up from the wool-covered seat on which she was sitting. She could tell by the mirror up front that her complexion was visibly darkening. What would she look like by the time they had traveled up to Hawk Ridge? Well, if they arrived all in one piece, Helia told herself, what she looked like would be a secondary worry. After all, soap and water could do wonders.

"Perhaps we should have lunch now," she suggested after several hours of jolting.

"I was wondering how far I'd be able to steer the car so I could keep on the road without something to eat," said Sadie.

Mother Gunda had packed a large number of sandwiches. When it was a question of attending to the appetites of young people pursuing an education, she was always happy to do her part. Helia had thought there would be enough sandwiches for supper too, but Sadie ate enough for three people.

"There's a real good restaurant in Hawk Ridge," Sadie said. "And everyone says it's real cheap."

Helia began to figure out just how cheap it would have to be to feed the three of them. If they arrived early enough, it might be possible to leave Netta at her home. They might even all be asked to dinner there, since they were giving Netta's parents a chance to see their homesick daughter.

When Helia had set out for college in the fall, her father had lent her his large Norwegian silver watch. "I go away from home so little," he said, "that our kitchen clock is all I need. All I ask is that you be careful with it and bring it back to me. It used to be my father's, you know."

Helia was glad that she had had the presence of mind to bring the timepiece along, since it gave her some idea of how they were progressing during the long, dusty afternoon. It was about five minutes of three when she noticed a peculiar blackness in the distance.

At first she thought it was a grove of dark evergreens bordering the horizon. But as they drove toward it, the dark line rose higher and higher in the sky.

The impossible was happening before their eyes. The sky was bordered by a bank of pitch-black clouds.

"It looks like it might rain," Sadie said nonchalantly.

Rain! The word had been the most precious one in the English language for more than a year. And Helia had thought that if it ever rained again she would be the happiest person in the world.

Yet now, of all times.

"You'll be all right on the rural roads," the attendant at the gas station had said. "Even though they're being worked over now. But if it should rain they'd be murder." But who, in this year of drought, ever stopped to worry about rain?

"Do you think we ought to stop and see what the weather turns out to be?" asked Netta timidly.

"No," Helia said quickly, feeling Hawk Ridge vanishing before she had time to get there. "If we're going to have to travel over wet gumbo, let's cover as much ground as we can before the rain comes."

They did not have long to wait. The solid bank of clouds spread over the sky just above them, and the black turned to a dirty gray. Then large drops began to show through the dirt on the windshield.

"If you find a good spot where we can get off the road," Helia told Sadie, "we had better stop."

She had scarcely finished speaking when the separate drops became a downpour, and Sadie had barely got the car to the side of the road when a deluge descended upon them. The rain was a white sheet all around them, and the roar was so great it was useless to speak.

Fortunately, Sadie's old car had a hard top, and it was only after a time that there began a gentle dripping inside. The leak was close to where Sadie was sitting, and since she didn't seem to mind, Helia held her peace.

The rain stopped as suddenly as it had begun. The clouds that had formed a heavy ceiling above them disappeared as if by magic, and the late afternoon sun again sent its hot rays down upon them. Except for the pools of brownish water here and there, there might not have been a downpour at all.

Sadie set her engine going and tried to turn the car into the road once more. The rear wheels spun without moving the car an inch. At last, after cramping the wheels from side to side, Sadie accelerated the car slowly and carefully. It gave a reluctant groan and then, barely gaining traction, inched onto the road again. After the torrents of rain, the gumbo had become as sticky and slippery as half-kneaded bread dough.

Helia watched while Sadie struggled. If she had ever felt any doubts about Sadie's ability to control the car, they vanished now. It was nothing short of miraculous the way she kept it moving, though at a snail's pace.

Sadie took off her coat and hat and handed them to Netta with one hand so that she could keep the other on the steering wheel. Helia could see the splotches of sweat darkening the back of Sadie's green dress.

"I wonder how far we'll have to keep on this," Sadie remarked rather than asked.

"We aren't far from Hawk Ridge, that I know," Netta answered timidly.

"Well, now we *are* in for a real picnic," Sadie said suddenly.

Just ahead of them were the bulldozers and other machinery that were being used for road construction. Eight or ten men stood on the side of the road. Helia

strained her eyes to see how bad road conditions were—
they *were* bad. The wet road had been plowed up into
deep grooves, and small streams ran parallel with its sides.

"Do you think we can get through?" Sadie called out to
the men.

"That's a question I wouldn't want to answer," one of
them replied.

A tall man who seemed to be the foreman came over to
the car.

"Do you really have to get by here today?" he asked.

Without waiting for anyone else to speak, Helia said,
"Yes, we do. No matter if I have to crawl on my hands and
knees, I'm going to get to Hawk Ridge today."

The man scratched his head. "Well, if it's that important,
I guess we'll have to try and help you. But I warn you it
isn't going to be easy."

Several of the men had come up to the car by this time,
and there was considerable debate as to how they were
going to get the car through.

Finally the tall man gave directions. And it was evident
that although he was embarking on what he thought to be
an impossible task, he was willing to do what he could.

First, he asked the girls to get out of the car to lessen its
weight. Sadie refused. When she set out in her car, she
told them, she never parted from it until she arrived home
again. Also, she added, she could steer it better than any
man.

In the meantime, some of the men had been busy laying
planks over the water-filled ridges in the road, so that they
formed a kind of track for the car.

The word was given to start, and with almost breathtaking accuracy, and at an even slower pace than a crawl, the car began to move over the planks, while men in rubber boots waded through the muddy stream on either side and helped to steady it. The planks covered about the length of a good-sized city block, and to Helia it seemed hours before the car was safely through.

"Good work!" one of the men called out.

The tall man approached Helia. "Since you are the one who absolutely has to reach Hawk Ridge by night, you had better go first."

Helia had once seen a performer in a circus walk a tightrope. Now, as she put one foot ahead of the other on the narrow plank, she thought she would have preferred to try that to walking the planks. The wheels of the car had left a covering of gumbo over the narrow boards, so that her feet slipped rather than moved over them. The boards slipped too. However, she had one distinct advantage over the circus performer. The tall man in his rubber boots walked at her right, and whenever she felt herself teetering he steadied her in a firm grip.

Just behind her came Netta. The walk over the slippery planks seemed endless. There was gumbo all over her shoes when she finally reached the car, and it seemed dreadful to drag so much mud into it. The flooring inside matched the outside now.

The foreman brushed away their thanks. "There's a dirt road that crosses the one just ahead," he told Sadie. "Better turn off on that. It's a roundabout way, but I don't think they had the downpour in that direction. Anyway, dirt roads are better than gumbo even when they're wet."

When they turned into the main street of Hawk Ridge,

it was far too late to drive to Netta's home before the interview. So Helia directed them to the restaurant, which, she said, was owned by the president of the local school board, and where she was to meet him.

It was a small, modest place—a counter where cold drinks were sold and six or seven tables out front. Whiffs of something frying came from the kitchen in the rear.

Netta went up to the counter and spoke to the man behind it. He said the owner would be back soon. In the meantime, Helia had no choice but to ask both girls to have supper with her. The place offered fried potatoes and hamburgers and coffee and dessert for fifty cents.

The three were still at their table when a man entered the restaurant, spoke to the counterman, and then came over to them.

"My name is Johnson," he said. "Iver Johnson. I'm president of the local school board."

Helia sprang up. "I'm Helia Singstad from Nidaros College," she said. "I believe the college has sent up my credentials." The hot meal had fortified her, and she was glad that she had taken the time to wash her face and hands thoroughly before they sat down. She could not help the mud on her shoes, but in general she hoped she made a good appearance.

"We were all much impressed by your credentials," Mr. Johnson said.

It was worth all the trouble they had endured, Helia thought in relief. *The job is as good as mine.* She remembered that the secretary had impressed upon her that she must be most businesslike about terms.

Then Mr. Iver Johnson stroked his beard slowly. "We

were just about to sign you up," he said, "when the treasurer of the board reminded us how short money was this year."

Here it goes, thought Helia. She could feel a pain beginning in the lower part of her stomach.

"He reminded us that Melina Olson was just out of college and that we could hire her for fifteen dollars less a month because she would be staying home with her parents. Not to mention the fact that the rest of her pay would most likely be spent right here in town, too."

Helia thought the room was going dark, and she sat down suddenly.

"It's too bad you had to make the long trip for nothing," Mr. Johnson was saying. "How about an ice-cream sundae on the house?"

Helia declined, and it was only Sadie Hunter who availed herself of the proffered treat. She managed to consume two, one chocolate and one with a mixed flavoring of butterscotch and caramel.

"Come on," she said to Netta. "We'll take you home now."

The Mellums lived on the edge of town in a white two-story house with a brave attempt at a lawn surrounding it. A tall, lanky, sandy-haired man stood in the doorway to welcome his daughter.

"It was good of you to give Netta a ride," he said. "Come in. Come in."

They were ushered into a room off a tiny hall. It was sparsely furnished but scrupulously neat. The detail that most impressed Helia was that, in spite of dust storms, here was a house whose mistress kept up the struggle of having clean lace curtains at the window.

When Mr. Mellum returned he said, "My daughter told me all about your disappointment. I'm both angry and sorry. It's really the fault of everyone in town that things at our school are run the way they are. Only a handful of people attend the school-board meetings, and if anyone gether and they sign up for him.

"The reason Iver stays on the board is clear enough," Netta's father continued. "If the teacher wants to stay in his good graces, she eats at the restaurant. And as for the treasurer, the Olsons are his second cousins."

A small, slight blond woman entered the room and greeted them, and Helia recognized her at once as Netta's mother. Without waiting for the girls to say anything, Mr. Mellum started explaining matters to his wife.

"I heard they need a teacher over at Three Oaks," Mrs. Mellum said.

"That's a small town," said her husband, "and they haven't got a high school yet. But that up-and-coming Don Sanderson is running the school now, and he would be a good man to work for."

"My brother is on the school board there," Mrs. Mellum said. "Why don't you call him right now?"

Netta's father went to the other side of the room and turned the crank on the wall telephone. "Give me Jens Bergen," Helia heard him say.

They had a long conversation, and then he came back to where Helia was sitting on the couch.

"My brother-in-law says that as far as he's concerned he'd be glad to hire you on our say-so. I'll get hold of those papers your college sent here and send them to him to-morrow."

"You are very kind," Helia said. "Will you let me know what the board decides?"

"You don't have to wait," Mr. Mellum said. "My brother-in-law is arranging a meeting of the school board over the telephone. We'll be having a ring as soon as they get together."

Mrs. Mellum brought in cookies and coffee, and the five of them sat around talking. Suddenly there was a sharp ring from the telephone, and Mr. Mellum told Helia to come with him. Most likely one of the members of the school board wanted to interview her.

Helia waited with shaking knees while Mr. Mellum lifted the receiver. He listened for a moment and then said, "The telephone operator is arranging for a board meeting over the wire."

He stood with the receiver at his ear, Helia standing close by.

"You are ready? All right."

Then followed a clicking, which Helia took to be conversation on the other end, interspersed with short comments from Mr. Mellum.

"About an hour ago."

"She'll get her diploma this spring."

"I'll ask them."

Then he explained that Mrs. Wilson, the clerk of the school board, was also on the line, and felt she would like to meet Helia in person before she hired her. Could the girls stay over Sunday?

At once Sadie Hunter rose up from her chair on the other side of the room. "We can't possibly stay," she called out. "I have to be back in Wheat City by six o'clock tomorrow evening. We'll have to start first thing in the morning."

Mr. Mellum repeated the information into the telephone receiver, and then there were more disconnected words. "You did? That's fine."

He turned to Helia. "That was Don Sanderson, who is the principal or superintendent or whatever you wish to call him. He was down at Nidaros College to hear *The Messiah,* and he recognized your name at once. He says you are exactly the kind of young woman they would like to have."

Helia was almost in tears. It seemed too good to be true. She had a job for next year.

"I couldn't pin him down on your salary," Mr. Mellum said. "But you can depend on him and Jens to give you a fair deal."

As soon as the matter was settled, Sadie Hunter spoke up once more. They would have to start at four in the morning, she insisted, since they were taking the longer way back to avoid the gumbo. Mr. Mellum said he would map out a route for them so they would have no trouble.

By the time the school-board meeting was over, it was close to midnight. Sadie thought it was foolish to try to go to bed at all, but Mrs. Mellum made up a bed for them on the floor of the parlor.

It seemed to Helia that they had scarcely lain down when the alarm clock went off and Sadie was on her feet. She wanted to start then and there, but it required little to persuade her to wait for the eggs and coffee and bread and butter and apple jelly which Mrs. Mellum served them on the kitchen table.

The sun had not yet risen when they departed for Wheat City.

"We're going to need gas and oil," Sadie said. "I hope there's a gas station pretty soon."

Though they found one after a few miles, it was closed, and a notice on the door said that it would not open before six-thirty on Sunday morning.

"We'll just have to wait until he arrives," Sadie said. "I don't dare risk waiting until we get to another."

Helia dozed in the back seat until Sadie woke her to ask for the money. "It's going to cost more than we thought," Sadie said, "since we're taking the longer way back."

Helia bought three candy bars. She had suddenly realized there would be no way of getting lunch. She now had sixty-three cents left.

The morning dragged on endlessly. The sun beat down unmercifully. The shower the preceding afternoon had raised the humidity and made the heat even more oppressive. But Sadie refused to stop and rest.

"I've got a date," she confessed finally. "He always comes to dinner Sunday evening, and I think I've got him to the point of proposing to me. If I'm not on hand, I might never have another chance."

They ate their chocolate bars in silence. Clouds of dust rose up about them as they rode along. But finally Helia began to recognize familiar landmarks.

"Well, I guess we're going to make it after all," said

Sadie, and she began to sing, " 'There'll be a hot time in the old town tonight.' "

Suddenly the car began to wobble.

"You had better slow down," Helia told her. "I think you have a flat tire."

It was all too true. The right-front tire had lost most of its air by the time Sadie stopped the car.

"Now what will you do?" Helia asked.

"Take the tire off and get to the next garage on the rim," said Sadie grimly. "Mother will start dinner for me, and I can wash at the kitchen sink."

They found a garage at Hazel Dell, and Helia pushed her purse at the attendant. "It's all I have left," she told him. "Do you suppose you could be kind enough to repair the tire for that?"

"Seeing it's Sunday, I guess we'll be easy on you," he said, and Helia was almost too exhausted to thank him properly.

They arrived in town so late that Sadie could not take Helia back to the dormitory, and she had to walk the rest of the way. She had never been so embarrassed in her life as she made her way through the town, dusty and dirty and caked with mud. The fact that it was Sunday and many people were out walking only made matters worse.

She had hoped to enter the dormitory through the back door and into the kitchen so that she could slip upstairs without attracting notice. But the back door was locked, and there was nothing for it but to walk around the building to the front entrance.

Vespers were held every Sunday in the dormitory parlor,

and they must have just ended, for to her horror people were coming out and standing on the steps. What should she do? There was nothing for it but to get inside as quickly as possible.

She reached the door and opened it, hoping to sweep by without stopping to be recognized, when someone called her name.

It was Dean Estvold.

"We were becoming worried about you," she said. "We heard you had started out yesterday on a long ride."

Almost in tears, Helia hurried past her without a word. Once inside the building she ran across the hall, tore up the stairs, and rushed into her own room. She slammed the door and was about to throw herself down on the bed when she realized how filthy she would make it. So she stretched out at full length on the floor.

After she had been lying there for a while, it occurred to her how comical she must have looked, and she burst into uncontrollable laughter. She was still lying on the floor and laughing convulsively when Dean Estvold entered her room.

"I got the job!" was all Helia managed to say.

Two weeks later, Helia met Netta Mellum on the campus and stopped to thank her for all her father had done.

"Have you heard anything more about Sadie Hunter?" Helia asked.

"Oh, yes," Netta told her. "My landlady attended her wedding last night."

HELIA looked anxiously at her reflection in the mirror on
Easter morning. This was the day that Dr. Winters was
paying his visit to her parents, and everything had to be
perfect. He had not forgotten the invitation her father
had extended to him on the evening of the Christmas
concert.

For the entire week Helia's heart had been in her mouth
whenever she thought of the impending visit, and that
was in almost every waking moment. It was hard to know
what Dr. Winters and her family would think of each
other. Also, everyone on the campus had heard about the
trip, and she had come in for no end of teasing.

Oivind offered to hide in the trunk in case a tire needed
to be changed on the road, and Lillemor asked to have
a good word said for her so that she would pass her
Shakespeare exam; but Peter Leegaard said nothing until
late Saturday night. Then he looked at her earnestly and
said, "Be sure to come back to us, won't you, Helia?" She
had taken Oivind's and Lillemor's teasing without being
bothered too much, but for some reason she felt her face
grow hot at Peter's words.

Last night she had sponged and pressed her light-blue

wool dress, basting down the pleats in the skirt before covering it with a damp cloth and bearing down with the iron as hard as she could. It had taken many coats of polish to give the illusion that her shoes were new. At least she never had to worry about her hair. A good shampoo and a brushing kept her natural curls in place.

Helia gave one last look at the mirror, seized her threadbare but decently neat coat from the bed and decided not to take her antiquated straw. As a protection against too much wind while driving, she carried a blue chiffon scarf, recently acquired at a rummage sale held by the literary society on the campus.

Dr. Winters was to come for her at quarter-past ten, and Helia settled herself close to the window in the north parlor so that she could watch for him.

Finally she saw the dark-blue Plymouth pull up slowly in front of the dormitory entrance. Her first impulse was to jump up and run down the steps as she would have done if any of the college boys had come to pick her up. But a student could not do that with a professor from the East who had come to take her home for an Easter visit, so she kept her seat and waited sedately for him to enter the building. Then she rose and walked slowly over to the entrance hall.

"Good morning," he said. "At least the weather is a little kinder than usual today."

As he stood there, wearing a dark-blue spring topcoat and carrying a gray felt hat, she thought he was one of the handsomest men she had ever seen. And as they walked down the steps together and he helped her into the car, she felt a little like Cinderella. There was scarcely a sound from the engine as they started for the outskirts of town. Helia couldn't remember when last she had ridden in a car that didn't make odd noises.

"It is pleasant to have the sunshine," said Dr. Winters. "I have given up hope of ever seeing rain out here."

Helia couldn't think of anything to say to this. It wouldn't have been very interesting to him, she thought, to tell him that she minded the drought as much as he did.

But she couldn't just sit like a bump on a log. "I have certainly been enjoying our Shakespeare class," she finally volunteered.

That was all that was needed. From then on, over miles and miles of straight roadway, Dr. Winters held forth on the subject so dear to his heart. Only, this time he talked about the plays he had seen and the famous actors. He had met the Barrymores, and his father had been an acquaintance of Richard Mansfield. He told anecdotes about E. H. Sothern and Julia Marlowe, and described how great actors had portrayed famous scenes. He talked on and on, and Helia sat spellbound. She could hardly believe her eyes when she finally realized that they were almost home.

Looking once more at the familiar places, Helia's heart sank as she realized the utter devastation that the past year had wrought. During Thanksgiving and Christmas it had been so cold that she had stayed indoors, and the landscape was always lifeless in winter. But now spring was here—at least, according to the calendar—and there was not the slightest sign of the awakening in nature there should have been. The rest of the family had been living with the disaster from day to day, but as Helia looked at it she could have wept. There was nothing left of their lawn but dead bushes and lifeless brown grass. The evergreens were dark and rusty. There were no healthy pine needles to indicate that life was left in the high hedge that protected their place from northwest blizzards, and nothing but a muddy hollow showed where there had once been a brook.

The whole family was outside to greet them as they drove up.

"It's a beautiful, beautiful day," Helia's father said, "and ready made for Easter. And now, as soon as we get some rain, things will be fine once more."

"Do come in," said Mrs. Singstad. "You had a long trip and you must be hungry by now."

As soon as Helia stepped indoors, she realized that tremendous preparations had been made for their coming. Even the storm windows had just been washed. Her mother had brought out the tapestry of The Tree of Life and hung it up on the south wall the way it had been before the drought. There was a delicious aroma from the kitchen, and Helia knew that in some way her mother had managed to get hold of a chicken or two.

"We weren't sure just when you might arrive," Mrs. Singstad said after their wraps had been removed and Dr. Winters was seated in the comfortable armchair that was usually reserved for Helia's father. "So we hurried back from church and I got dinner real early."

"Yes, but Mother, you remember—" her father suggested.

"Of course. Does the professor take wine?"

Dr. Winters looked dubious but agreed that a little wine might be all right. However, once he had tasted the home-made wine, he did not have to be urged to take a second glass.

Helia's father asked about the trip out, and Dr. Winters answered, but not too eloquently. As soon as her mother could get the food ready she invited them to the table. It was not the lavish Sunday dinner they had known in other years, but Dr. Winters seemed to enjoy it.

"The boys and I will take care of the dishes," Mrs. Singstad said after it was over. "You go in, Helia, and visit with your father and Dr. Winters."

Frankly, Helia would have preferred to stay with her mother in the kitchen. But it was not fair to leave her father alone to entertain the professor.

"I have been much impressed with the resourcefulness of you people in Dakota," said Dr. Winters politely. "It is hard to see how you can have the courage to remain on your farms."

"Oh, this isn't the first time there has been a shortage of water out here," Helia's father said. "I remember the year I was twelve it was almost as bad as this."

Dr. Winters seemed interested, so Helia's father continued. His father and mother had come from Norway when they were a young couple and had taken out what was called a tree claim—they had got the land almost for the asking by promising to plant so many trees an acre on the level, empty prairie. There was not a bush to be seen when they arrived, and for a long time not even a single bird.

It was good land, Mr. Singstad explained, once water was applied to it, and his father had the gift of sounding for water, and soon they had a well.

"As I said, we had a drought the year I was twelve and the well went dry, so we went to a neighbor's to bring home buckets of water. While we were away my mother saw flames in the distance. The tall prairie grass was as dry as tinder, and there was no way of saving the house or the barn. She saved her own life by jumping into the dry well, but she hurt herself so badly that she was never able to walk again. That was a hard year, because my father died of pneumonia the following winter."

"I should think you'd have had enough of pioneering by that time," said Dr. Winters.

"Not my mother. She had my brother and me fashion a sort of seat with handles on both sides, and we would carry her about the place and she would decide what ought to be done. She was a very small person, and my brother and I were easily able to carry her."

"But with no buildings, nothing—how could two boys manage?"

"My father had built a shack the fall before he died, and we lived in that through the winter. One end was separated by a makeshift partition, and we kept our horse and cow in there. Fortunately, we had taken the horse to the neighbors, and the cow we had bought on credit."

Dr. Winters sat silent.

"The neighbors gave us a barn-raising in the spring, and my brother and I traded work until we had a chicken coop and a granary. Every year we made some sort of an improvement on the farm. Mother saw to that, and finally we got a windmill to pump water from deeper wells that can never go dry. So we always have drinking water, at least, and even in a drought we can keep some things alive."

Dr. Winters shook his head. "I simply couldn't keep my faith with such setbacks."

"Oh, there have been dry years and wet years. The dry years have been temporary, and always the good years have permitted us to forge further ahead than we were before the droughts came. Let me show you over the place, and you'll see what I mean."

Dr. Winters got his coat and Helia put on a sweater, and as they walked around the farm Helia tried to look at it through her father's eyes.

"As far as the ground itself goes," said Mr. Singstad, "it doesn't hurt it to remain fallow for a year or two. We have the best soil—once there is moisture—of any state in the Union."

"But isn't it discouraging," asked Dr. Winters, "to have to start all over again?"

"These fruit trees will have to be cut down," Mr. Singstad admitted, "and it will take some time before the new ones are ready to bear. But Mother is thrifty, and preserves all she can every time there is a good crop, so we always manage to have all we need."

Helia wished her father wouldn't go into too much detail about the farm. Dr. Winters surely would not be interested. But she loved the place as much as her father did, even if she found it hard to be as optimistic as he was.

"Now, these apple trees are alive still," her father said. "Theodore and Edvard have been carrying water for them. In the future, when I get more wells dug, I'll be able to save more trees when another drought comes. As for the dead trees on the place, they will at least keep us in fuel for a long time."

"I don't see how you can remain so hopeful," Dr. Winters said.

Mr. Singstad chuckled. "Suppose in your teaching you found a class with which you had worked hard, and which failed to come up to your expectations. Would you then and there give up your profession?"

Helia was genuinely surprised and more than a little proud of her father. Usually he seemed almost naïve in his approach to anything with which he was not familiar, and his attitude toward learning was so reverent that she had not expected him to challenge Dr. Winters so directly.

Dr. Winters smiled. "With your attitude toward South Dakota, you should be employed by some chamber of commerce out here."

"Dad, don't you think Dr. Winters would like to go in again now?" Helia suggested.

"Perhaps you are right," Mr. Singstad agreed. "After all, Mother will be wanting to visit with Dr. Winters too."

After they arrived back at the house, her mother served them coffee and jule bread. This was originally a Christmas delicacy, but the Singstads always had it on special occasions. This time the raisins and orange peel were missing and her mother had obviously economized on the eggs. But Helia and her brothers enjoyed it thoroughly, and she hoped Dr. Winters was not merely trying to be polite when he ate two generous slices.

"A drought has many compensations," said Mr. Singstad. "For instance, our boys have been able to work

much harder in school this year, since there was no farm
work for them to do."

"I spelled down everybody in my room," said Norman
suddenly.

"You've already told me that," Helia said, and laughed.

"Want me to tell you all the hard words I know?" said
Norman. "Megalomaniac, troglodyte, chiaroscuro."

"That's enough from you," Theodore told him.

To change the subject Helia said, "How are you getting
along with your braided rug, Mother?"

"It's all finished," her father said eagerly, "and it's a
beauty. Perhaps Dr. Winters would like to see it."

It was laid down on the parlor floor, oval in shape and
with wide stripes in various color combinations. It was
plain that Dr. Winters was very much impressed with
it.

"Mother can do anything with her needle," Mr. Singstad
said. "When I met her she was working in an exclusive
dress shop in Minneapolis, and before that she was employed to sew for the very best people in her home town
in Norway."

Helia began to feel uneasy. Would Dr. Winters feel that
they were a family of boasters? Or that they were merely
trying to compensate for the terrible drought and its effect
on their way of living?

"I'm afraid I'll have to take my leave now," Dr. Winters
said finally. "You know, all country roads look alike to me,
and I have to get back to Wheat City before dark."

"Oh, but the road you take is different from all the
others," said Norman. "It's graveled all the way, isn't it,
Helia?"

"Yes, it is. But where Dr. Winters comes from, all the streets are paved."

"Boy, I'd like to take a ride in a place like that!" Norman said.

"Perhaps you will someday," the professor said. "It has been a real treat for me to be welcomed into a home like this. I don't know when I have had a more pleasant day."

"It was very kind of you to give Helia a ride home. And we hope you come again," said Mrs. Singstad.

The whole family went out to see Dr. Winters off, and then the three brothers went to do the chores, it being a tradition in their home that their father was always free on Sunday nights. Helia and her mother cleared the table and washed the dishes while her father studied his precious *Farmer's Almanack* near the fire burning in the kitchen range.

"Father," Helia's mother said, "I am wondering whether the professor might not have thought us a little boastful."

Helia's father looked up. "What makes you think that?"

"Well, you taking him around the farm, as if to show him how large a tract of land you owned. Then—well, you said so much about my skill in sewing and made me take out the rug. Not all men are as interested as you are in such things."

Edvard had come in with a load of wood. "Yes," he said, "and Norman spelling out all those big words like the professor didn't know them and a million others."

Mr. Singstad put down his pipe. "Dr. Winters came out to see us because he is interested in the way we live in South Dakota. All that is a part of the way we live."

"I wish there could have been some flowers in the house,"

Mrs. Singstad said. "Perhaps we should have brought back the geraniums we took to the church for Easter."

"But I thought you and I agreed to leave them for Mr. Gudmundson's funeral tomorrow. They will mean a lot more to his sorrowing relatives than they would to Dr. Winters."

"I guess you're right," Helia's mother conceded.

"It must be interesting for a scholar like Dr. Winters to be a witness to history actually being made," Helia's father went on. "In the East everything is finished, but out here things are still new. South Dakota is a young state, and we Norwegians have pioneered out here. In the East he has attended universities that were more than a hundred years old, but at Nidaros he is helping to build a good college."

Helia got up and gave him a hug. "I'm very proud of you and all my family and the house too."

Her father picked up the *Almanack* again. "And do you know," he said, "I was just reading that the drought will be over by the middle of May."

ON THE first of May, Helia thought despairingly, I guess people are right when they say we ought to give the land back to the Indians.

Ever since she had come back from Easter vacation, she had thought about the prophecy in the *Farmer's Almanack* and the desolation of their once-beautiful farm. Until then she had never been so conscious of the drought or found it so hard to endure. Even indoors she could feel the grit under her feet, and outdoors it was everywhere—she breathed it, tasted it, felt it in her eyes and nose and ears.

Without realizing it, she had counted the days to May, and when the new month finally arrived she jumped out of bed and ran to the window to peer hopefully at the sky. Her window faced west, and for a moment her hopes rose. There seemed to be just a suggestion of gray on the horizon. But, no, it was grayish blue—only the presence of dust, the eternal presence of dust that dulled everything.

Each morning after that, she went to the window as soon as she woke up, and each day the dust was there.

On the fourth day she didn't have to bother to go to the window to learn about the weather. She could hear the wind whistling, the sand beating against the windowpane, the creaking of the rafters. It was another of the storms that never brought rain. Well, wind or no wind, she would have to get ready for classes.

Only a few more days now, and they would be over. Over forever as far as she was concerned. And what a desolate campus her parents would be coming to for commencement! She was almost tempted to write and ask them not to come. But that would be unthinkable. Ever since her first day she had pictured the triumphant moment when her family would see her getting her diploma at college.

The next day the wind died down, and when Helia examined the horizon she thought she saw a real cloud. She took hope, dressed quickly, and hurried down to breakfast to announce to those at her table that she thought it was going to rain. As the morning went on, there were more of the same gray clouds. But by noon they had become lighter and skirted toward the south and finally disappeared.

On the morning of May 6th, when she awoke it was dark. She looked at the clock; it said seven. There must be some mistake. She got up and looked out the window and saw that heavy clouds were covering the sky. She opened the window, and there seemed to be a dampness in the air. But no. Not a single drop wet her hand. She closed the window. Would it ever rain again?

Down in the dining room there was an atmosphere of excitement. One of the students had been out on the steps of the dormitory and said she felt a few drops of rain. No, she was not dreaming. These were real, wet drops. Another girl went out to confirm the story and came back with several spots on her light dress to prove it.

After breakfast, the students hurried upstairs and out the front door. The rain was coming down in a soft patter. Some of the girls stood on the sidewalk and let it drop over them. One girl said she was just going to stand there until she was soaked to the skin, just to make sure she was not dreaming.

Classes went on that day, but no one paid much attention to them. The students kept their eyes on the streaming windowpanes. Helia felt that nothing else really mattered now. The rains had come. She could think of nothing else.

The steady downpour continued, not violent, but in ample volume. All night she lay listening to the sound of it against the windowpane. Several times she got up, opened the window, and put her head out to let the rain fall on her.

It rained all the next day and the night following. On the third day the skies began to brighten, but still the rain fell, lighter now but persistently.

Gradually the appearance of the landscape began to change. First, there was a suggestion of green on the ground. Then more green and then the actual appearance of grass. The buds on the trees began to swell, and they grew green too. The bushes began to look like something more than bare sticks.

Within a week, the campus gave promise of the arrival of spring. There was a fragrance in the air of growing grass, leafing trees, spring flowers. The world had suddenly become alive and beautiful.

By contrast the campus itself looked shabby. There had been no way to keep out the fine dust that had sifted in through the cracks of the windows and had ground its way into everything. Outdoors, some of the plants and bushes had died, and refuse had settled around others—paper and rubbish that would normally have been cleared away. It would take a fine combing to get rid of the sand that covered so much of the grass and choked the young shoots now rising from the ground.

Old Nils could not possibly perform such a huge task, and the college had no money to hire people from outside to come and clean it up. Yet everyone wanted the campus to look as fine as possible for commencement.

Finally the student body held a mass meeting to discuss the subject. Peter Leegaard presided.

"We have all felt apologetic about the appearance of our campus," he said. "But now that the trees are coming out and the birds are returning, I wonder whether all of us couldn't do something to help."

To Helia's great surprise, it was little Netta Mellum who rose first. "I think, since we freshmen have the largest number of students in our class, we ought to take on the largest job. And I think it would be fun."

"And what do you consider the largest job?" asked Peter.

"The grounds, of course. We could make it an all-day picnic affair, and with all of us working I'm sure we can get a lot accomplished. If we aren't through the first day, we'll keep at it until we are."

Helia thought of the brave attempt at a lawn in the Mellums' yard at Three Oaks, and of the freshly laundered curtains in their windows.

She rose. "I think we should offer the freshman class a vote of thanks."

"Better wait until we find out if her classmates agree with Netta and want to do it," said Peter.

As if at a signal, all the freshmen shouted, "We will! We will!"

Not to be outdone, the sophomore class took on the cleaning of the gymnasium. The parents and other close relatives of the seniors were invited to stay on the campus, and the gymnasium was used both as a dining hall and as a dormitory for the visitors.

Oivind Otness then spoke. "The chapel will need a lot of attention. I move that the juniors get it into tiptop shape for both the baccalaureate service and the commencement exercise."

The dormitory was left to the seniors.

The freshmen started in the very next morning, and shortly after breakfast the grounds were alive with talking and laughing young people. Helia had no classes for the day since she was preparing for her final examinations, and she could see the activity from her window. She was so fascinated and amused that she found it hard to concentrate on her work.

Old Nils was in command, and he was assisted by Peter and Wilhelm, who had taken the day off to help.

The freshmen worked in teams of two and three. Some raked, some picked up bits of paper and other refuse, some carried bushel baskets. Old Nils had a large group untangling paper and other windblown objects that had settled among the roots of the bridal wreath and honeysuckle hedges. When the roots had been cleared, some of the sturdier boys hoed the ground around them. Old Nils let only his most trusted assistants help him trim the bushes and the trees. Strangely enough, there had been few casualties. The college had an ample supply of wells, and Old Nils had had the foresight to water the bushes heavily late in the fall.

Mike was everywhere and enjoying the fun. Someone put the handle of a small hoe in his mouth, and he walked about as if he too were working. After a while he let it go, tossed it up in the air, and then took it over to one of the freshmen. However, when two students put a rope harness on him and tried to get him to pull a heavy basket of grass and refuse, Mike would have none of it.

Mother Gunda served lunch out on the grounds. Everyone seemed to be having such a good time that Helia almost wished she were a freshman again.

Helia was busy with examinations the days the sophomores and juniors conducted their part of the clean-up campaign, and it was only after the work was finished that she saw what they had accomplished. It must have been a tremendous task, reaching up to the rafters in the gymnasium and getting at the upper part of the walls. But they shone, and so did the floor. Cots had been brought in, and a huge table was piled with blankets. The boys and men who came to town for the commencement activities would sleep here the two nights they spent in Wheat City. Nidaros did not have dormitory accommodations for the men students.

As for the chapel, Helia had forgotten that it was such an attractive place. The lectern, the pews, the varnished woodwork halfway up the walls, and even the pipe organ had been given a thorough cleaning and polishing, and although the windows were only plain glass, each pane gleamed.

The seniors waited until the lower classmen had left

before they began to prepare the dormitory to house the mothers and sisters who were coming to Wheat City. The girls took charge of cleaning the second and third floors, while the boys assumed the responsibility for the parlors, halls, and the Dean's office. They also washed all the windows, though Old Nils insisted on supervising that operation. "We aren't going to have any broken bones at this celebration," he told them.

The morning of the seniors' workday dawned bright and sunny, and the girls all appeared at breakfast in their oldest work clothes. To their surprise Marion Fletcher put in an appearance just as they had started in the rooms on the second floor.

"I told Daddy that I wanted to show you girls from the country that a city girl knows how to work too."

And she certainly kept her word. Sleeves rolled up and hair tied back, she began taking a bed apart with Helia's help, scrubbed it, and returned the mattress to the springs. She did her full share cleaning woodwork, walls, and furniture, and by noon she and Helia had five spotless bedrooms to their credit.

"Mother Gunda sent word for everyone to come down to lunch," Lillemor said.

And it was a lunch for hungry workers—potato pancakes, scrambled eggs with strips of crisp bacon, applesauce, and all the coffee anyone could drink.

"That's the way I like to see people eat," said Mother Gunda, as she sent in platter after platter. "It shows that you appreciate my cooking."

After noon the boys came up to tackle the upstairs windows.

"I never dreamed that I would be given entrance to this sanctum," said Wilhelm Otness.

"Industry brings undreamed-of rewards," Lillemor teased.

"I'm glad I didn't major in housecleaning," Helia said. "My bones are beginning to squeak, and my muscles are so sore I can scarcely move."

"I called Daddy and asked him to pick me up," Marion admitted. "I could never make it back home on foot, and I'm going to get a good rubdown tonight. But I wouldn't have missed this for anything."

At the end of the day Bodil and Lillemor sat in Helia's room nursing their aches.

"I don't see how I'm going to hobble around at class-day exercises tomorrow," said Lillemor. "Even my toes ache, I'm that tired."

"Same here," Bodil said. "But anyway we did a good job, and I can't wait for Mother to come here and stay the two nights. It's going to be loads of fun."

"I don't know if I've got enough energy to get down to the dining room for supper," Helia said.

"Believe me, I can get down to the dining room," Lillemor said. "It will be absolutely heavenly to sit at a table and have someone wait on me after jumping up and down forty times a meal to see that five children are properly fed. But I'll bring your supper up to you afterward if you like."

Helia accepted the offer gratefully. After supper the girls went straight to bed, and next morning they all agreed that they felt fine again—except for being conscious of muscles they had barely known they had.

It was then Helia saw for the first time what the boys

had achieved downstairs. The chandeliers sparkled and the lamps looked brand new, so carefully had the metal and shades been cleaned. The boys must have brushed both ceilings and walls. The floors were scrubbed and waxed, and the upholstery, without its coating of dust, revealed its original color. The tables and chair frames shone like mirrors, and, best of all, the place smelled clean in a way that it hadn't since before the drought.

Helia's parents were among the first to arrive.

"I don't think Norman slept a wink last night," said Mrs. Singstad. "And he just can't wait to give you his present."

Norman smiled self-consciously, but he at once handed Helia a rather crumpled paper bag.

"Now what do you suppose that is?" Helia asked.

"Look and see," said Norman.

To her surprise she took out of the bag a whistle made from the sturdy stem of a willow.

"Try it and see if it works," said Norman.

Helia drew a deep breath and pressed her lips to the opening. The result was a shrill sound that could be heard over the entire dormitory.

"He wants you to have it so that you can call your classes to order when you go out to teach," said Helia's father. "I have no doubt it will be useful."

Helia turned to Norman and kissed him. "It was awfully nice of you to make that whistle for me."

"Aw, shucks," said Norman, pulling himself away. But there was a broad smile on his face.

"We certainly appreciate being invited to stay here as

guests of the college," Mr. Singstad said to the Dean, who had come up to join the group.

"The students have more than paid for their parents' visit by their splendid work," said the Dean. "We are very proud of the fine appearance of the buildings and grounds."

The most important part of the day to Helia was the presentation of the gift to the college from the senior class. It was a linden tree, which was planted just in front of the Ibsen administration building where every student would see it many times a day.

Wilhelm Otness dug up the first spadeful of earth to cover the roots after his brother Oivind had placed the sapling in the hole, and it was Marion Fletcher who made the presentation. But this time she was not chosen because of the elegant clothes she would wear. She had become popular with everyone in her own right, and Helia was proud to have her as a friend.

"We are happy to present this linden tree," she said, "and we hope it will encourage others to think of ways of beautifying this wonderful college and its surroundings."

On Sunday morning, Helia accompanied her family to the college chapel where the baccalaureate services were being held. The seniors sat in the choir seats, and she could see the entire audience. She looked with pride at her family seated in the front row. Just behind them were the eight young Otness boys. Helia had never seen them all together, and as they made their way down the aisle, tall, large-boned, and preceded by their stalwart parents, she thought they looked like young Vikings.

There were white lilies and roses at the altar—a gift from

Marion Fletcher's father. The congregation sang with fervid enthusiasm "A Mighty Fortress Is Our God," and the minister spoke the first verse of the Nineteenth Psalm:

> "The heavens declare the glory of God;
> And the firmament sheweth his handywork."

Helia was moved by the psalm as she never had been before, and she felt tears on her cheeks.

There had never been such a beautiful morning in South Dakota, she told herself as she and Lillemor and Bodil walked from the dormitory to the entrance of the administration building where the commencement procession was to assemble. There was a bright sun with just enough of a breeze so that she was not too warm in the academic gown she was wearing over her white piqué skirt and voile blouse. And there was a fragrance of growing things all about that made her want to sing with happiness.

Several members of the faculty were already on hand in their academic regalia, and so were the members of the band. A considerable number of onlookers had arrived early—women holding babies in their arms, small children tugging at their skirts, girls, older boys and men.

"I was beginning to think my partner in the procession wasn't coming," Marion Fletcher called out.

"Not a chance," Helia answered her. "It's the most important day of my life, next to the one on which I was born."

"Let's start to line up," ordered Professor Koppang of the German department, the marshal of the event. "You know President Presthune likes to have everything start off on the minute."

Although there was much small talk during the assembling and some low laughter, there was an air of subdued happiness quite unlike the seniors' usual noisy bantering. The band began the first chords of "The War March of the Priests" from *Athalie*, and even though Helia had been expecting it she gave a start. As they moved toward the chapel she was torn by a series of emotions—pride and humility; reverence and a sense of satisfaction that she would now be earning her own money; joy and a great sadness that this was her final day as a student at Nidaros.

As the procession entered the chapel, the audience inside rose and turned toward them. The band gradually muted its sound so that when the last graduate had reached his seat up front, the music gently died away.

Helia listened closely as the Reverend Norlien asked God to bless these young people who were now leaving their alma mater to make their way in the world. He prayed that they might have the wisdom to make good use of the training that they had received in this fine, though young and small, institution. She joined heartily in the singing of "America the Beautiful," but when the guest speaker, a prominent educator from Illinois, began to read his speech called "America Needs Her Youth," her thoughts began to wander.

It would have been more interesting, she thought, if he had told the audience the story of how Nidaros had begun. Of how ministers in their itinerant travels around the little communities on the frontier had told the settlers about the school that was being put up by the Norwegians, and had urged all able-bodied men to help. Her grandfather had walked the entire distance from his land to Wheat City, and had been one of those who helped drive the nails in the first building. The women had gathered money through the Ladies' Aid to pay the teachers, and the books had been the gifts of the early ministers, most of them in the Norwegian language.

Suddenly there was a general movement in the audience and a rustling of programs. The main speaker had left the lectern, and in his place were President Presthune and Mr. Sverre Nordland, the president of the board of directors. Someone was placing a bundle on the lectern.

The time had come for the presentation of the diplomas. No more daydreaming now. She was not going to miss hearing her own name called when it was time to go up to the lectern.

"Oivind Oliver Otness."

Helia watched Oivind leave his seat and climb the two steps up to the platform.

"By virtue of the power invested in me by the Board of Regents of Nidaros College, I hearby grant to you the degree of Bachelor of Arts."

One by one the names were called, and in the case of Bodil the president changed his wording slightly. Instead of merely granting her the degree of Bachelor, he added *cum laude,* and Bodil's hands were shaking as she went back to her seat carrying the precious diploma.

Helia was beginning to wonder whether her name might have been for some unforeseen reason omitted when suddenly it came loud and clear: "Helia Marie Singstad."

Her heart beat fast as she walked up to the president. She hoped she wouldn't trip on the stairs. Somehow things seemed blurred, as if her eyes were not functioning properly, but she got to her destination without mishap.

She was sure she could not have heard correctly what President Presthune was saying, *Magna cum laude*. The only student ever known to achieve this distinction was Orville Henderson, and he was a brilliant young man who was now studying for the ministry.

But she must have heard correctly, for when she got back to her seat Marion Fletcher, who was sitting next to her, squeezed her hand so hard that it hurt.

There was only one other graduate to be summoned, President Presthune said, but he was not the last in rank. He had earned the highest honor that had ever been bestowed upon a graduate of Nidaros College—*Summa cum laude*. Not only that, but he had been awarded a fellowship of a thousand dollars by the Great Eastern Chemical Corporation for graduate study at the university of his choice.

Helia felt the tears trickling down her cheeks as Peter Leegaard made his way to the lectern, and after the benediction had been said and the ceremony was over she went up to him and kissed him on the cheek. Then she immediately regretted her impulse, for Peter turned bright scarlet.

Helia's parents and three brothers came up to her, and Edvard, usually the silent one, blurted out, "Well, we're going to have a *magna* living with us this summer!"

The crowd gradually filed out of the chapel until only Helia and her family were left. When she was at the door she turned and looked back. To her surprise she saw Peter standing up front all alone. No one, not even his father, had been present to share his honor.

Helia whispered something to her mother, and she spoke to her husband. Immediately Mr. Singstad hurried to Peter's side, and Helia heard him say, "Peter, Mother and I would like you to be part of our family today."

And the two came arm in arm down the aisle together.

Helia knew, as she sat at the table in the dormitory, that she would remember every detail of that day. But most of all she would remember the sweetness and love her family were showing to Peter as they did their best to make him feel one of them.

> And what is so rare as a day in June?
>   Then, if ever, come perfect days;
> Then Heaven tries earth if it be in tune,
>   And over it softly her warm ear lays:
> Whether we look, or whether we listen,
>   We hear life murmur, or see it glisten. . . .

HELIA yawned, and stretched luxuriously at full length on her bed. Her clock said it was a quarter to eight, but she made no move to get up.

She had stayed at Nidaros a few days to help Mother Gunda do the housecleaning, and now that that was finished she had the day to herself. Mother Gunda was leaving early in the evening for Montana, and by that time Helia would be at home. Peter had asked her to go with him on a picnic, and after that he would take her to the bus depot.

She was looking forward to seeing the farm again. Her father had told her that since the rains had come, it seemed as though the whole farm had wakened into life. It made Helia think of the story of the sleeping princess, when the prince arrived at the castle and everything came to life. The brook was full of water again and singing over its stones; some of the apple trees had blossomed; and now that the danger of dust storms had passed, her father and older brother had been able to do the spring plowing. Helia could almost smell the damp, freshly upturned earth.

When Helia finally arrived in the kitchen she was greeted with a most inviting aroma of coffee and fried bacon, and she saw that pancakes were in the making.

"I'm ashamed to be so late," she told Mother Gunda.

Mother Gunda was pouring batter into the hot pan. "Oh, you need have no scruples," she said. "I guess you've worked hard enough these last few days."

Helia looked around for Old Nils.

"He was here hours ago," Mother Gunda said, "and so was Peter Leegaard. Nils asked him to meet him here at quarter-past six this morning. You can never account for the way Old Nils does things. It seems he had a gift to present to Peter, and he didn't want any of the other students to know about it."

"What was it?" asked Helia.

"It was a camera. Of all the things I ever heard, the most unlikely is that Old Nils would go shopping for a camera. And you should see what an elegant one it was."

Mother Gunda served up a batch of pancakes. "Old Nils sets store by many of the boys and girls, but he really loves Peter as if he were his grandson. He said he supposed Peter would be going off to far places, and he wanted him to take pictures and send them back so he would know how he was making out."

Mother Gunda set down the coffeepot in front of Helia. "There was so much foolishness going on I nearly didn't get Old Nils' lunch ready for him. Every day he has five double sandwiches and a quart thermos of coffee. That's one of the things I worry about when I'm at my sister's home at Montana in the summer. The maid they have here is good, but there are certain things about Old Nils that, no matter how much I impress them on her, I don't think she remembers."

"But can't Old Nils remind her?" Helia asked.

"No, he won't. He just gets moody and cross. But to go back to the foolishness. As soon as Peter and Old Nils had finished breakfast, Peter said the first thing he wanted to do with his camera was to take a picture of Old Nils, and such a smile came on that man's face as I never seen in all the years I've known him.

"And nothing would do but that I go out and watch the performance. Such nonsense," she added, pretending to be disapproving. "I wanted Old Nils to go to his room and put on his coat and a respectable hat, but do you think he would? He said he wanted the picture to show him when he looked natural. Then Peter wanted to take my picture— dressed as I am for work. I told him a flat no. I don't want him to carry the memory of me as an old drudge, even though I have been one a good part of my life. I told Peter to come along someday when I'm dressed for church and I'll let him snap as much as he likes."

Helia burst out laughing.

"Old Nils grumbled about females being nothing but peacocks, but when it came time to take Mike's picture that animal had more sense than Old Nils. He sat up straight as a movie star, and I declare there was actually a grin on his face."

Helia was humming as she went upstairs again. She was glad she was spending her last day with Peter, and perhaps he would like to take her picture too.

She looked in her mirror. Yes, her hair lay in soft ringlets about her face. It was a great advantage to have naturally curly hair. She was wearing the same white voile blouse and cotton skirt she had worn for graduation. She picked up her bag and gave one last look around her room before she left it.

After she had said good-bye to Mother Gunda and Old Nils, she settled down in the north parlor to wait for Peter. He was usually early, and should be along very soon.

As she sat looking out the window, she was surprised to see Dr. Winters coming up the walk. She had thought he must have left town by now. Since she was the only one in the dormitory, she got up from her chair to open the door.

"I was hoping to find you here," Dr. Winters said. "I had heard you were still in town."

He looked very elegant in a light gray suit, but somehow younger and less like a professor. Helia could not feel the awe of him that she had during the school year when she was his student.

"Won't you come in and sit down?" she said.

"I can stay only a few minutes. But an idea has occurred to me that I thought might interest you."

He sat down, and Helia looked at him full of curiosity.

"I might as well come to the point at once," Dr. Winters said. "At first when I came out here I was greatly disturbed by the poor facilities, especially the inadequate library. And I was also disappointed in my students. But as the year wore on I took heart, for I was amazed at what could be accomplished with so little. I was especially pleased with you, Miss Singstad."

Helia was too surprised to say anything.

"So the idea came to me," Dr. Winters went on, "that I might be able to do something for you. I have some connections, and I should be most happy to recommend you for a fellowship to one of the larger eastern universities."

Helia felt her heart beat fast. It sounded almost too wonderful to be true. She would travel, and go to all the interesting places in the East that she had heard Marion Fletcher mention so often. She would receive an advanced degree, and there was perhaps no limit to how high she might go in her profession.

She was about to tell Dr. Winters how happy she would be to accept his kind offer, when suddenly she knew that she couldn't.

It would mean, for one thing, that she would not be earning any money next year, and she knew how many sacrifices her family had made for her already. Apart from anything else, she had set her heart on seeing the money in her mother's copper kettle begin to accumulate again.

And then there was the school at Three Oaks and the students who were expecting her there. She had promised to make it possible for them to get a start on a high-school education by teaching as many subjects as she could that would count toward a diploma. Suppose they heard that she had changed her mind because something more to her advantage had come up?

She spoke without hesitation. "It is very kind of you, Dr. Winters. But I have my plans made for next year, and it would not be possible to change them now."

Dr. Winters showed his disappointment. He rose and

held out his hand. "I'm sorry," he said. "Perhaps if I had had the idea earlier, we might have worked out something."

Helia could not tell him that it would really have made no difference. She knew what she was going to do, and she would be happy in doing it. "I do want to tell you how much I appreciate your thoughtfulness. It was most kind of you."

"Perhaps some time later you may find it possible," he said. "And remember, I shall always be pleased to help you."

After he had left, Helia picked up her bag and went out on the front steps. Peter arrived almost at once. He was wearing a white sports shirt and blue trousers, and she thought he had never looked better. In fact, Helia thought him very handsome.

"You look pretty enough to have your picture taken right now," he told her. "And then I'll have one of you with the dormitory as background."

Helia posed for him smiling. Then Peter picked up her bag and they started to walk to the bus depot to leave the bag in the locker. When they arrived, Peter took complete charge, finding a locker, placing the bag in it, locking it, and then putting the key in his wallet.

"Suppose you lose it?" Helia suggested.

"Then you'll just have to stay in Wheat City the rest of the summer."

Helia had never known Peter so lighthearted.

"Are you going to leave your camera in the locker too?" she asked.

"I should say not."

"But you took my picture up at the college."

"I know. But I may want to take another."

He piloted her out of the crowded bus depot and they started up the street.

"Where are we going now?" Helia wanted to know. "Or is that a secret, too?"

"I'll tell you," said Peter. "We're bound for a delicatessen."

The woman behind the counter seemed to know Peter. "I have your lunch packed," she said, "and with all the extras you ordered."

She returned with a huge box, and Helia's eyes widened. "You really are planning to keep me here all summer," she told him.

They caught a bus, and Helia realized they were on their way to Pettigrew Park on the outskirts of town. "I used to come out here often," Peter said, "after I had been sweating it out at the laundry."

The park was already crowded, but Peter seemed to know exactly where he wanted to go. Finally he stopped under a huge elm with wide spreading branches. There he set down the box on a small picnic table, and Helia offered to help him open it.

"No," said Peter. "I'll manage everything."

On the top of the box was what seemed to be a layer of white crepe paper.

"I see Rose has followed my instructions to the letter," said Peter, unfolding it, and Helia could see that it was a white paper tablecloth. He spread it carefully over the table and then proceeded to take out the rest of the contents of the box.

There were buns with thick slices of baked ham in them,

and Peter had even thought of the sweet pickles that Helia liked so much. There were big wedges of chocolate cake and paper containers filled with double milkshakes.

"Even though I had a good breakfast, I'm starved," Helia admitted as she sat down.

"How do you like my cooking?" Peter asked finally.

"It's perfect," Helia said as she took her last bite of chocolate cake and finished her milkshake. "Won't you let me take care of the cleaning up?"

"A good host takes charge of that, too," said Peter.

While Peter put away the paper cartons and other litter, Helia looked about her. He couldn't have chosen a more beautiful picnic place, she thought. It was almost at the brink of the bluff just above the Indian River. The caretakers of the park had done a fine job of cleaning up the grounds after the long drought, and there was a carpet of green grass under the tree that shaded the table.

Peter returned.

"And now what?" Helia asked.

"I want to take your picture under this elm," Peter said. "The light is just right."

She posed for him under the elm and then by a birdbath and then sitting on a rustic bench.

"Now it's my turn to take your picture," said Helia, getting up.

"I've used the last of the film," said Peter, closing the camera and sitting down on the bench himself. "Come and sit beside me here for a little while."

"That's not fair," said Helia. "I want your picture, too."

"The people who are giving me the scholarship have written for a picture. If it turns out, I'll send you one."

"Promise?"

"I promise. But I expect you'll forget about me in a little while."

"I couldn't do that," said Helia.

"I know what happens at small places when there's a new girl in town. Especially when it's a pretty new teacher. Everyone flocks around, especially the young eligibles. And with you, the prettiest girl Three Oaks will ever have seen—"

Helia felt her heart begin to pound.

She sat very still. Peter moved closer to her on the bench.

"Helia?"

"Yes."

"Do I have a chance? Will you wait for me?"

A warm feeling surged through her entire body. "You know I will," she said.

Peter put his arm around her and drew her close.

"This is the happiest moment of my life," he said, and kissed her.